P9-CQA-719

DO NOT REMOVE FORMS FROM POCKET

CARD OWNER IS RESPONSIBLE FOR ALL
LIBRARY MATERIAL ISSUED ON HIS CARD

PREVENT DAMAGE - A charge is made for
damage to this item or the forms in the pocket.

RETURN ITEMS PROMPTLY - A fine is charged for
each day an item is overdue, including Sundays
and holidays.   JUN 1 1 1991

REPORT A LOST ITEM AT ONCE - The charge for
a lost item includes the cost of the item plus a
$5.00 non-refundable service fee.

 LOS ANGELES PUBLIC LIBRARY

The Shepherd Moon

the shepherd moon

a novel of the future by
H.M. HOOVER

THE VIKING PRESS, NEW YORK

VIKING KESTREL

Viking Penguin Inc., 40 West 23rd Street, New York, New York 10010, U.S.A.
Penguin Books Ltd, 27 Wrights Lane, London W8 5TZ (Publishing & Editorial) and
Harmondsworth, Middlesex, England (Distribution & Warehouse)
Penguin Books Australia Ltd, Ringwood, Victoria, Australia
Penguin Books Canada Limited, 2801 John Street, Markham, Ontario, Canada L3R 1B4
Penguin Books (N.Z.) Ltd, 182-190 Wairau Road, Auckland, 10, New Zealand

Copyright © Helen M. Hoover, 1984
All rights reserved
First published in 1984 by The Viking Press
Published simultaneously in Canada
Printed in the United States of America
by Arcata Graphics, Fairfield, Pennsylvania
Set in Garamond No. 3
3 4 5 6 7 91 90 89 88 87

Library of Congress Cataloging in Publication Data
Hoover, Helen.   The shepherd moon.
Summary: When a colonist from a forgotten artificial moon returns
to earth, thirteen-year-old Merry and her grandfather must
battle to save their culture from the visitor's strange powers.
[1. Science fiction]   I. Title.
PZ7.H7706Sh   1984   [Fic]   83-16784   ISBN 0-670-63977-X

FOR ROSIE

The Shepherd Moon

chapter 1

ON A HILL ABOVE THE SEA STOOD AN ANCIENT HOUSE. BUILT
in the forty-third century and typical of that period, it was a
sprawling warren of wings, with bubble-capped towers, tracery
bridges, and gardens dead or gone wild. Tall trees blocked tower
views. Ivy fed on crumbling walls. Every rain brought the house
closer to the sand from which it had been spun.

South of the house, beyond the gardens and shielded from
view by trees, were the barns and what remained of the greenhouses. There the fields began.

Where meadow ended on a tip of land that overlooked the
sea was a stone bench. Two people sat there in the October
dusk. One was a woman of thirty, the other a girl of thirteen.
The woman was waiting for the world to change. The girl wanted
to see the moonrise.

Tonight's moonrise was a special thing. There would be five
full moons. This happened once every eighty-nine years. Few
people lived to see it twice. The four small moons were man-
made, although man had forgotten that. Civilizations had come

and gone since those colonies were built, one by one, until more than ninety space habitats circled Earth like a string of beads.

In ancient days when men still dreamed of traveling deep into space and usurping planets of other, distant stars, the *moons* were built as steppingstones into the future. They were public works projects, as awful as the pyramids. Like the pyramids, they employed the best technology of their time, but their time passed and their purpose was forgotten.

Now, in place of knowledge, myths explained the satellites. Some called them Children of the Moon. Others said they were rocks flung out from Earth by giants in the past. They were believed to be powerful and evil, racial memory thus retaining hints of historical fact. Their rising was thought to cause insanity and chaos. Babies born beneath the moons were watched carefully for abnormal behavior.

"There were cities out there, where the water is now," the woman said, breaking a long silence. "Long ago. The oceans were much lower. People lived along the coast." She shifted to cross her legs and close her cape over her dark uniform.

The girl looked at her expectantly, politely. She'd heard the story many times, but few would have guessed so from her manner.

"They say when all five moons are full the tide goes out so far that ruins rise above the waves, and every time that happens, old things are washed free."

The girl shivered in spite of the skeptical glance she gave the woman. "What kind of old things?" she asked.

The woman gestured impatiently, as if details were unimportant. "Valuable things—gold, jewels, all polished by the waves. Some wash ashore. And old bones, skeletons—"

"I don't think so," the girl said doubtfully. "They'd have to have been there for more than five hundred years. My books say that as the ice caps melted—"

"Water preserves." The woman nodded agreement to her own beliefs. "The sea's full of salt. And there's no air down there. The servants say their parents and grandparents found things you wouldn't believe." Then, anticipating awkward questions, she added, "They sold them, of course, long ago—they didn't say exactly what they were."

"Oh." The girl turned her attention back to the sea. The tide was going out. Water was slopping and sloshing over the seaweed-wracked shingle. Far to the south towering clouds suggested rain was coming.

"This is stupid, you know, sitting out here in the cold when you could watch from inside where it's warm." The woman stood up and scanned the area behind them, then pulled up her hood and blew on her hands to emphasize her discomfort. "You could see just as well from a window."

"No." The girl, whose name was Merry, didn't like the woman much, but then she seldom liked bodyguards. No one she knew did. Bodyguards were constantly watching, listening, intruding, seldom doing what they were hired to do. When no adults were around, they tended to be bossy and take social liberties they wouldn't dare to otherwise, like sitting with her on the bench instead of remaining at a distance. And they all expected her to be grateful for their presence, including this one, Worth.

The two eyed each other, each through her own prejudices. The woman was tall and powerfully built, although her dark uniform made her look smaller. Her brown hair had gone fuzzy in the sea wind, bushing out and making her face look even more like a bright-eyed potato. She outweighed Merry by a hundred pounds, and her strong hands could have crushed a throat with ease. There were tales of mad bodyguards who'd turned on their employers. Merry sometimes thought of those stories when she looked at Worth.

The woman saw just another child, featureless—her job. At

least this one was polite, but then quite often her type used
manners to mask contempt, as this one's parents did. But that
was part of the job, putting up with their attitude. At least the
pay was good and the living quarters better than most. For that
she could put up with listening to this kid whose idea of casual
conversation was telling you about some stupid old book she'd
read or some boring fact she'd learned. But then most members
of the ruling class were a little crazy.

"You can go back to the house, Worth. I'm perfectly safe.
I've been here"—she paused to count—"four months now.
Nothing's happened, and it won't."

"You know I can't leave you outside alone."

"Yes, you can. You have my permission."

The woman gave a contemptuous sniff. "A lot of good that
is. I don't know why I agreed to come to such a deserted place,"
she complained. "There's nothing to do but eat and sleep. The
only good thing is there's nowhere to spend money, and no one
to spend it with. These local people aren't much brighter than
their machines. But then, isolated as they are, they've probably
intermarried." She laughed at her own joke.

Merry got up and walked down the cowpath along the cliff.
Sometimes a person was less lonely alone than with someone
like Worth. She didn't understand Worth and didn't want to.
The woman's presence was the price she'd paid for coming here,
on her father's insistence.

At home she lived in the secured section of the city, a parklike
enclave of buildings on the hills above the river. There the huge
houseboy, Bishop, served as bodyguard when necessary—which
wasn't often, since her school was nearby and she seldom had
reason to go into the open part of the city. But the servants
had gone with her parents and, in any case, Bishop wasn't much
better company than Worth. Her parents' choice of employees
was quite deliberate, she knew—to keep her from becoming

attached to servants, a thing they frowned upon.

Her parents were to pick her up on their way home. She'd been expecting them for more than a month now. School had started, and she would fall behind. If something had happened to them, surely someone would have told her. If only they'd left permission for one of the staff to fly her home!

Instead of going with them on their yearly cruise, she had chosen to spend the summer here at Easthaven, her grandfather's country home. Adolescent moodiness, her parents said. But she had studied hard that year and grown five full inches, and she was tired. The idea of being sociable to her parents and their guests for three long months was more than she could face.

As spring came and the city warmed, she'd found herself thinking about this house, remembering a time when she was four and brought here to meet her great-grandmother, an old woman said to be eccentric, living in total seclusion. Merry hadn't found her odd. They had stared at each other with the long, hard stare of infants and hunting animals; neither said a word. She remembered the woman's thick white hair, her brocade dressing gown, and her cold, dry fingers as she touched Merry's cheek and then gave her a gold ring with a beautiful dark green stone with smoky feathers in its heart. Her mother had taken the ring for safekeeping—Merry couldn't remember what became of it— but she still remembered the immense quiet of the place, and the greenness, and the animals, and the long flight to reach it all. Her great-grandmother was gone now, but the estate hadn't changed. It was still as peaceful as her memory.

The waves made a scallop of foam lines as they rolled in. A tern hung in the air, a graceful silhouette of a bird. Far out on the horizon the lights of a freighter were pinpoints. No ship of any kind ever came near this shore. There were too many drowned ruins thrusting up, hidden by the waves.

After a plump and rosy babyhood that had earned her her

nickname, Merry had begun to stretch into reedy adolescence. She had fine dark hair and eyes already slightly saddened by awareness. She was aware, for example, that her parents had liked her better as a small child, for then they could regard her as they did their dogs, but with a special tolerant fondness because she was the brightest of the pack. As she grew older and gave evidence of their waning youth, they grew less comfortable with her. She was old enough now to guess they would never quite approve of her again, but she lacked the experience to understand why or accept it.

That she did well in her studies was of little interest to them. She'd come to understand that here. If anything, they were disappointed that she wasn't more socially inclined. Her winning a scholarship did not thrill them. In fact, they seemed to find it in rather poor taste, since that sort of effort and achievement was important only to those who had to work for a living. They did not. Few members of the ruling class did.

She came from a family whose members, over the centuries, had married with great care and did not divorce. By following this custom, the Ambroses had kept and always added to their wealth and power—if not always their honor.

Once, when she was small, she'd overheard her father say that she was a "nasty little bother and boring besides," and her mother had laughed and said perhaps they "could leave her somewhere." Ever since then Merry had made an effort to be well-informed so that when she liked people they wouldn't want to leave her. Perhaps she'd overdone it? But it was difficult to tell how interesting one was if others were polite.

To be honest with herself, she thought, trotting down a steep slope to the beach, she *was* interested in things that most people like her parents and their friends found boring. She always had been. Like watching the moons come up. Or finding that this house, Easthaven, had vaults of ancient books in the cellars beneath the library. That was why she liked school so much; there were people there—not many, admittedly, but a few—who shared some of her interests and didn't think her odd for having them.

Like Ben. The two of them had counted 1783 separate species of insects to be found in the courtyard garden at their school—and had made everybody nervous with the news. And Nina, with whom she played piano duets and who sat next to her in every class and lived two floors below—but who refused to say they were best friends because, she said, you couldn't count on things lasting. Nina's mother had been married five times. Merry grinned at the thought of them both. She'd wanted to ask them here for a visit, but her parents had said no, that if she wanted company, she should come with them.

She heard Worth's footsteps on the path but didn't look back. The lights had come on in the house and barns. All the staff were indoors. They said that walking in the light of the moons brought bad luck. She wasn't sure they believed that, since no one had tried to discourage her from coming out.

When the big moon rose, she was down on the beach, walking along the shingle and wishing it were light enough to see what the outgoing tide might be exposing. Worth was still behind her, up on the sand, and every few minutes she called a suggestion that they go inside where it was warm. Merry was quite cold by now but determined. "I think if it's something important," she called to the woman, "you should see it clearly if you can. Not secondhand, through glass or in a picture."

"What difference does it make? It looks the same."

It made a big difference, Merry knew, but she couldn't explain why, and she walked faster to get away from Worth's muttering about her stubbornness.

She couldn't really say she saw the little moons rise; they were just suddenly *there* when she glanced away to the northeast. Where the big moon was a rich warm ivory, the little moons were a cold gray-blue. They looked about a fourth as large, but she knew they weren't, that it was their close pass by Earth that made them seem so. She had seen them in pictures, but the effect wasn't the same. There was something about them that made her shiver, like seeing a bad omen in the sky. Then she realized part of what was wrong.

"Worth, look!" she called excitedly. "One of the moons is missing!"

"Who cares?" came the reply. "They're just ice balls, anyway. Can we go in now? I'm freezing!"

The autumn rains began at noon. Wind gusts shook the trees. By early dusk leaves were down, whole branches dark and bare. Paths washed into shallow gullies. The ancient landing pad west of the house became a pond.

Merry hardly noticed. She spent the day trying to learn what could have happened to that moon. The computer in her study was no help at all, listing the smaller satellites as ". . . probably the remnants of an ancient meteoroid trapped in a fixed orbit, they are believed to be composed of ice and stone." There was one curious picture, captioned "View of the Solar System, Circa 2870," which showed Earth with only two moons, one large, one small. She assumed people hadn't known any better two thousand years before. Yet Jupiter and Saturn were shown with the correct number of moons.

That night she was awakened by the purring of a giant cat, a sound so distant and enormous it seemed to fill the room, the house, the world outside. She came up slowly from deep sleep, aware of the rhythmic throbbing. It was not frightening so much as it was curious. She couldn't imagine what it was.

She turned on the light and listened. The perfume bottles on the dresser were dancing on their silver tray. The lampshade whispered a hoarse vibration. When she reached back and pressed her hand palm-flat against the wall, vibrations traveled to her elbow—and with them fear. Less than a minute passed between her waking and getting up. Raindrops ran down the windows, but she couldn't hear them strike the glass; the purring drowned out their sound.

In her bathroom the water in the toilet bowl was swaying. She stared down at it and wondered, *Earthquake?* She'd never felt an earthquake, only read about them. She stepped out in the corridor to listen. No one else was up. She considered waking people, then decided not to. They might be angry if there was no danger or, worse, might laugh at her.

Small flames still flickered behind the fireplace door, and sparks flurried up the chimney as the andirons shook. As she put on boots and a raincoat over her pajamas, an ember exploded with a crack so loud that she stumbled against the closet door in fright.

On the ground floor she tiptoed down the main corridor to a small side lobby. With the outside door open, the purring was much louder but its source no more apparent. She stood in the doorway listening, half afraid to go farther. The air smelled cold and sweet. She shivered and wondered if she should go back and dress, or would the house collapse? Remembering that animals were supposed to sense earthquakes, she set off for the barns, hugging her coat to her, her head down against the scattering rain. The wet ground squelched at every step, but she couldn't feel it moving.

The dogs began to bark before she reached the stock barn, and when she opened the door they greeted her with touching gladness, pressing so close that she nearly fell over them. She patted them distractedly, wishing they could talk. Bo and Bernie were dignified dogs under normal circumstances, but now, like herself, they seemed to want reassurance that something wasn't terribly wrong. A quick tour of the big building revealed most of the animals were awake but unfrightened; even the riding

11

horses were calm. So maybe it wasn't an earthquake? Before leaving the stable, on impulse she dropped to her knees, pressed her ear against the brick floor, and listened. One of the dogs sniffed her hair and sneezed.

The purring wasn't coming from the ground. It wasn't the slow, rumbling bellow of a deep-layer quake, but a steady, even throb in the air, as if from a laboring engine. Perhaps a ship was in trouble. That would explain why it didn't advance or recede in the distance.

The dogs ran with her down across the sheep meadow to the shore. Mushrooms had sprouted, dotting the field with pale white spots. The rain clouds were plainly visible now, high and glowing with strange orange light, like the smoke from a forest fire. As she stood, head back, blinking against the rain, the purring noise abruptly stopped and she could hear the surf again. Her ears popped, and the dogs both whined as if something hurt, then acted apologetic when she asked them if they were all right.

The sky grew brighter until she could see layer upon layer of heavy clouds roiling overhead, trailing dark wisps and billows and folding in among themselves. The choppy surface of the sea became visible and faintly orange. A bright thing like a huge winged maple key drifted out of a cloud and fell in a slow, twirling motion down and down to disappear behind a crest of waves. Then a shapeless dark thing fell, then another, until it occurred to her that perhaps she should seek shelter under a tree in case something fell her way. But the clouds were getting still brighter, as if something were coming down through them.

The dogs bolted and ran for the barn. She didn't even notice. With the calm of wonder she stood and watched an enormous fiery mass shoot out of the clouds at meteoric speed, hit the sea halfway to the horizon, roll, and disappear. From somewhere far off came a sharp, massive crack of thunder or an immense sonic boom.

There was a sound that could have been the hiss and curl of a particularly large wave and then stillness before the wind suddenly bent the trees all to the south and blew her flat on her back in the wet grass. She was knocked silly for a few minutes, and when she could think again, the night was almost normally dark except for a special darkness out over the water.

By the time she got up and brushed off her coat, she was engulfed by fog. She turned around, looking for the lighted windows of the house and barn, then turned again, preoccupied by shock and the fact that she was wet and cold and her head hurt from the fall. She couldn't see any lights. She couldn't see her feet in their white boots, or her arms. She held up her hand and couldn't see it even when it touched her nose. She had no idea in which direction she was facing. "So this is what they mean by blinding fog." She spoke aloud, hoping the sound of her voice would convince her she wasn't afraid. It didn't help; she was badly frightened.

A big wave struck the beach below and was followed by a larger wave. There was a lull and then a third poured in louder than any she had ever heard. The fog diffused the sound so that she couldn't tell where the beach was but knew the cliffside was less than twenty yards away—in some direction.

"Bo?" Her voice was like a plaintive birdcall in a lull between the thunderous waves. "Bernie?" She tried to whistle, but her mouth wouldn't obey. "Bo?" After she had called for what seemed like ten minutes, something brushed against her leg, and she gave a little squeak of surprise. A wet velvet nose touched her hand, and she groped about, feeling head and ears, found and closed her fingers over a dog collar. "Let's go home now," she said. "Time to go home." After a hesitation there was a tug on the collar and the dog set off.

The walk back was all upgrade, over uneven pasture, and she stumbled often. Each pause on her part brought the dog to a halt, not sure what she wanted. Each time she would repeat, "Let's go home." The dog's tail would whisk against her coat and they would set off again. He could have led her anywhere; she wouldn't have known the difference. As it was, the walk took so long, or seemed to, that she began to suspect the dog couldn't see or smell his way either. The fog smelled of some chemical she couldn't identify, and breathing it left a nasty metallic taste in her mouth.

She felt gravel underfoot and heard its welcome crunch. They were going in the right direction, having reached a driveway. The dog stopped and wouldn't go on. After thinking things over, she reached out into the fog and her fingers struck a wall . . . a frame . . . a door! It opened onto the lighted tack room of the barn. It was so good to see again that for a moment she just stood there while the dogs pushed in ahead of her and gave themselves a vigorous shaking. Their shaggy gray coats were curled and matted.

The dogs weren't allowed up at the house or on the lawns, she remembered as she shut the door and dropped onto the groom's bench to rest. That's why they'd brought her here. She turned and peered at the window. Fog pressed solidly against the pane. She'd never find her way the quarter mile or more up the hill to the house. If she followed the drive and hoped to find the walks by foot feel . . . but that was too scary to risk. Her knees weren't all that steady now, and she was wet through and cold. She'd stay here till morning. The dogs were still shaking their coats, throwing silver droplets.

She got up and went in to the hay ramp, pressed the button and stepped back as she had often watched the grooms do. A big rolled bale came sliding down from the mow above. She pushed it into the tack room, put a quilted warmup blanket over it and two more to cover up with. There were clean towels in the grooms' locker. She hung her wet coat on a harness peg, took off her boots, and toweled dry, then crawled into her rustling makeshift bed. It smelled of horse and was somewhat scratchy but warm, or soon became so when the dogs curled up beside her.

She tried to make sense of what she'd seen. She thought it was a meteoroid, but she wasn't sure. It wasn't an airliner; none ever was *that* big. But the sonic boom . . . and what had caused the purring? Perhaps it was the missing moon? But its mass would destroy much of Earth.

Bernie yawned and sneezed and chewed a pesty stomach flea, then yawned again and closed his jaws with a little snapping sound. She yawned and patted both dogs. "Thank you for rescuing me," she told them. "Whoever it was. I couldn't see, you know. . . ." In seconds she fell into exhausted sleep.

chapter 11

WHEN FIRST LIGHT WOKE THE DOGS, THE RUSTLING HAY woke Merry. They whined to be let out. It was still raining and foggy, but things were visible again. Beyond the pines the house looked especially beautiful rising up out of the mist, as if it rested on clouds instead of being firmly planted on its hill.

As she stood at the stable door, her head began to itch. She scratched; timothy and clover chaff fell from her bangs and made her sneeze. On the other side of the wall the horses stamped and snorted, alerted by the human sound to the hope of break-fast. Rain blew onto her bare feet, and she shut the door.

The horses were a reminder that the stockmen soon would be coming in and would wonder why she had slept in the barn. Not that they'd ask; they wouldn't nor would she explain. But they would gossip about it later. Before putting on her boots and raincoat, she folded the horse blankets and replaced them on their shelves, then pushed the hay roll back beneath the chute.

Sea gulls were wheeling and crying along the length of the beach. She'd never seen so many, but then she'd never been out this early. They might be dawn feeders, or seeking shelter inland from the storm. Normally she would have stopped to watch, but the chill rain, combined with her scant clothing, made her hurry up the hill toward the comforts of a bathroom and hot water.

The house was quiet. If anyone else had been disturbed by the events of the night, there was no evidence of it. A rover unit was polishing the floor of the main entrance hall. Others were cleaning the corridors. The warm air smelled of wax and cleaner and yesterday's flowers dying in their vases. She went through the Yellow Hall, the Tapestry Hall, and the Mirrored Salon—great lofty rooms that were never used—turned left and climbed the inner passage to the second floor.

Such an odd old place, Merry thought later, as she dried her hair. At home she could have turned on the news and been told what she'd seen the night before—if it was important—but here there were no news or information channels, no electronic communication with the outside world. Great-grandmother had seen to that. The house computer was just that, limited to the house. Even its entertainment screens fed on archived dramas so old that they had been ludicrous a century before. But then the house was three hundred years old.

Once dressed, she made her way down to the kitchen. Breakfast wasn't served until eight, more than an hour away. Located on the ground floor, the kitchen was enormous, designed to serve several hundred people. She'd been shocked the first time she saw it, not realizing until then what this house must have been like in its heyday, the guests and support staff it had once served. Now of the kitchen's twenty cooking tiles only four were used, and one of its twelve ovens. Even with five sides of beef, two of pork, and several lambs, the coldroom was almost empty, as were the flour, rice, and vegetable bins. All food served was grown on this land. For both health and security reasons the ruling class ate only natural food (not the heat-and-eat synthetics the commoners preferred), and their kitchens required extensive equipment, storage, and preparation space.

In the bread keep was a tray of plump bran muffins. She took two. Hunting butter in the cooler, she discovered a bowl of eggs. She put two on to soft-boil, then looked for a plate, and, not finding one, made do with a handy pie tin. The eggs and muffins were washed down with a mug of milk, since she couldn't find the crystal. By seven she was walking down the meadow to the beach, glad to be outside and still free of Worth.

The sheep had been let out to graze. They huddled in a group at the south end of the meadow and looked none too pleased to be out in the mist and rain. A few were straggling back to their warm, dry shed, their bells tonkling as they followed the half-mad Nubian goat who was their guide. From the barn came a rooster crow, its cheerfulness denying the gloomy morning.

On the cliffside path she stopped and stared down at the beach, squinting against the wind-driven mist. Worth's story of things washing out of drowned ruins came to mind. The waves had cut a new cliff out of the sand below, and now, at low tide, several hundred yards of shingle lay exposed. Both shingle and sand were strewn with white things and broken tiderows of litter. She ran halfway down the muddy path before she realized the litter was dead fish and each incoming wave brought more.

"The meteor must have exploded underwater," she remarked to the world in general. "Poor fish!"

Flocks of gulls moved grudgingly out of her path, less afraid of her than the chickens were. The birds were breakfasting on everything from a gelatinous mass of jellyfish to crabs to a five-foot gray shark. A black ray was white belly up, its tail and eyes eaten away. A dead sunfish the size of a tabletop washed back and forth at water's edge. A school of infant herring spattered one stretch of rock like scattered coins. Among them lay barracuda, hunters and prey both victims. Brown kelp and green and red seaweed lay in tangled windrows. Even in the rain, clouds of insects gathered as greedy as the gulls to feast on tragedy.

Everywhere she looked there was something dead. With the aid of a driftwood stick she flipped over some of the bodies. Most showed no visible damage. Half the fish were species she'd never seen before. Square pillow-shaped black skates' eggs draped themselves in tangled little necklaces. Broken seashells tinkled like gravel as the waves rolled them back and forth.

After a half-mile walk she decided to turn back. For as far as she could see, the beach offered only more of the same. But then down near the chimney rocks some hundred yards away she saw what appeared to be huge black pillows piled up on the sand. Curious, she walked down.

They looked like skate eggs, but from a fish of monstrous size. Each egg was at least five feet square and three feet through the center. Their corners were tipped by the same curving claw-like hook. Four remained hooked together in one big tangle. A fifth pillow lay by itself, tipped against the rock, and even though the waves normally struck these rocks with great intensity, appeared undamaged.

"Why don't you eat these?" she inquired of the gulls around, who were feeding on smaller prey. "Or are you scared of them?" The birds ignored her.

The truth was, the size of the eggs was frightening. She could imagine how large the parent must be, and how large an infant shark might emerge from an egg this size. The case was big enough to hold her in comfort, with room for a friend if they curled up carefully.

She went over to inspect the single egg more closely, pulling away the kelp draped over it. The egg case suggested a rigid black plastic. But then the first time she'd seen skate eggs she hadn't known what they were until a gardener told her. And she didn't believe him until she took one to her study and cut it open, much to Worth's disgust. Worth wouldn't even admire the cleverness of them, the beauty of design, the efficiency in packaging. "I guess that sort of thing matters to your type," she'd said cryptically, "but to me they're just garbage that washed up on the beach. They stink and they're no good for anything." That was Worth's criterion for value: how a thing could be used.

As she was wondering what Worth would say to this one, the egg made a sharp hissing noise. She jumped back, but not quickly or far enough to avoid a very bad smell. The gulls took off, frightened. As she watched, a narrow line of white foam oozed diagonally across the middle of the shiny blackness. The foam increased and grew frothy. She wasn't sure, but she thought she saw the surface of the pillow buckle in and push out again. If a baby shark came out live and thrashed about . . . she imagined how far it could move with its egg sac, and she moved back farther, stepping carefully between dead fish and slippery kelp on the shingle. When she looked at the egg again, a second line of foam had appeared, forming an X. For minutes nothing happened while she watched and shivered.

Even with her hooded slicker over her sweater and slacks it was cold standing still. Rain dripped off her hood and ran down her sleeves into her pockets, where she kept her hands for warmth. Only her feet were cozy inside their high, pile-lined boots.

Then she noticed that the raindrops had no effect on the foam. They hit or ran into it, but nothing washed out. And that seemed curious. She was considering going back for a closer look when the foam began to steam. Wisps of smoke or vapor blew away on the wind, and when the smoking stopped, not only was the foam gone, but the X was an opening.

No egg behaved like that! She didn't know much about the sea or its animals, but she was almost positive no egg could do *that.* Some odd sort of bomb might. She scanned the rock behind her, searching for a quick way up . . . but the cliff overhung the beach here.

Ready to start running, she glanced back at the pillow thing in time to see something move inside it. A slender human hand reached out through a slit, paused to feel the rain, and withdrew. There was a person in there! She'd caught a glimpse of a tight yellow sleeve. The top flap was slowly pushed out, then the left, and after a long pause the right. She waited, hardly daring to breathe, as curious now as she was frightened. Nothing happened for a few minutes, and then above the wave noise she heard someone crying. It sounded like a child.

After hesitating a moment to argue with herself, she gripped her sturdy driftwood club and tiptoed close enough to peer inside the thing. A body lay curled up, arms hugging its knees, head down, shoulders shaking with sobs. It appeared to be wearing yellow tights that had been soaked in foam. Globs clung here and there. Its blond hair was wet and matted to its head. The smell escaping from the pillow was richly unpleasant.

Merry repressed a gag, turned her face into the wind, and backed away again.

"Are you very sick?" she called. The crying stopped in mid-sob, but there was no answer. Her grip on the club tightened. "Hello? Are you sick?"

The pillow shook and shifted on the rock. The lower flap pushed out and a yellow leg appeared, then a second leg. The tights encased the feet, like infant pajamas. Bare hands gripped the folds of either flap, and the person hoisted himself out. He was a tall, slender boy, almost a man. He tried to stand erect and swayed and reached out to clutch the egg case. It shifted, and he grabbed hold of the rock for support. Even though he looked dazed and ill, he was the prettiest person she'd ever seen, all golden and blond and smooth.

"Do you want me to go get help?" she called. "Can you walk?"

She saw him stagger as he tried to turn toward her, and help seemed a very good idea. If he couldn't walk, she'd never be able to get him back to the house by herself. "You wait here. I'll be back!"

"No! Don't go! Don't you leave me, too!" Tears ran down his face: a child in despair. If she hadn't seen him, weren't looking at him, she would have thought the voice came from a five-year-old. It was disconcerting, this voice from this person, and the thought occurred to her that he had gone crazy trapped inside that *egg*. Or maybe he had been crazy before, and someone had gotten rid of him this way. She gave the four remaining eggs a nervous glance. And so did he.

"I'll get help!" she promised. "Don't be afraid."

"Please don't leave me!" he begged. "I'll be good. Please!" With that he reached out to her, open-armed, the cloud glare making his beautiful hazel-green eyes seem brighter than they were. "I'll be good," he said again, and attempted a step toward her.

What would have been imploring from a baby was scary from an adult. Merry backed away. "You stay right there," she said nervously. "Maybe you'd better sit down? I'll be back with help."

"No! Please!" She heard him start to cry again, but then her running scared the gulls into flight and their shrill cries drowned out all other noises. She slipped several times on fish and fell, and once on the muddy path. When she reached the cliff top, she paused to catch her breath and decide whether house or barn offered the quickest chance of help. Deciding on the barn, she set off again, running as fast as she could.

If she had looked back, she would have seen, down by the chimney rocks, a small intense beach fire that gave off a thin vapor of oily black smoke. Beside it, a yellow figure hurried about, adding fuel to that fire. By the time Merry burst into the barn, the yellow figure was bathing in a tide pool.

chapter 111

SHE FOUND A MAN AND A WOMAN IN THE DAIRY PARLOR,
finishing the last chores of the morning milking. Merry didn't
know their names. They were surprised to see her, and a bit
amused by the mud all over her front, but as soon as she told
them about the stranger on the beach she had their full attention.
The woman left the last cow on the milker and went to the
intercom on a nearby wall.

"Intruder alert," she said. "Unknown male on the beach. Possibly four others. Last seen directly north of Boron's Rocks."
She called over to Merry. "Was he armed?"

"No. Just sick and smelly. He got seasick floating, I think. . . ."
She paused, wondering if she should mention that he might be
crazy. "He's . . . frightened and miserable, crying. He can't walk
too well. They better take a beach car."

"Are you all right, miss?" the dairyman asked as the woman
repeated Merry's story to the intercom. He tipped his head to
see her face under her visor and smiled.

"Yes, thank you. Just muddy." Merry pushed back her hood

and grinned at him. "As you probably guessed, I fell down. Don't tell Worth I'm out, please. She'll have fits and come after me in her bathrobe."

"They're going down to get him and search the beach for more," the woman said, coming back to her cow. The cow glanced around at Merry and mooed as if accusing her of interrupting. The woman flipped a switch, and the animal, released from the stanchion, hurried into the next room to join her sisters at the feed trough.

"Thank you!" Merry headed for the door.

"You shouldn't go near him," the man called. "Not until he's identified."

"I promised I'd be back," Merry said, "and I try to keep my promises."

A rescue team caught up with her on the beach, their open, fat-wheeled vehicle bouncing and sliding over debris. The car had come from the north side of the point where a driveway led down to an inlet and a long shed where kelp was processed. As the car came closer, she recognized three of the gardeners clad in slickers.

"You shouldn't be out here, miss," one said grumpily when she flagged them down. "It's dangerous."

"I found him," she reminded them. She climbed aboard the flatbed and tried to ignore their disapproving faces.

The driver shrugged and put the car back into gear. "Something unnatural in the storm last night," he said, changing the subject to save face. "In thirty-two years I never saw a fish kill like this. Not even from red tide."

"It was a meteoroid," Merry informed them, talking over the noise of the car and the screaming, swirling gulls. "It woke me up. Didn't anyone else see it?"

"I heard thunder," said one. "There was a lot of lightning."

"What's a meter rood?" yelled the driver.

"What exactly did you see?" asked the man who seemed to be in charge.

She gripped the roller bar firmly as the car bounced along, squishing fish and scattering birds. The men seemed interested in her story, but they interrupted too often with questions instead of listening, forcing her to repeat things. She wasn't used to talking in a yell.

"Something on the sand up there!" the driver called out.

Merry pulled herself to her feet and peered through the rain. "That's him! He must have tried to follow me. He was way over there—the pillows are gone!"

"Washed back out."

"They were too far up. There, by that rock." She pointed.

"We'll load him first, then look around." The driver stopped beside the body, which lay face up on the sand.

"He didn't have that cut on his forehead. Or that bruised cheek. . . ." Merry jumped down and crouched near him for a better view. "He didn't look hurt at all." He also smelled much less than he had, and his face was even more beautiful unconscious, expressionless.

"Here! Don't get so close! You don't know where he's been." The grumpy man deliberately stepped between her and the body so that she had to move and stand to keep from toppling onto the sand. She glared at him, but he ignored her, his attention on the stranger. They frisked him—too professionally for gardeners, she noticed—and then they took his pulse. When they started to pry open his mouth to check inside, she turned away and walked on down the beach to the rocks.

There was no sign of the pillows. The shingle seemed darker than she remembered, and cleaner. In fact, there were no dead fish, no gulls, nothing in a wide, ragged semicircle. She walked down to where the foamy water could lap her boots. Two flounders floated like dead leaves. Pieces of burned sticks bobbed and nudged her toes and then slid out again as the wave receded. One of the sticks was shaped like a thigh bone. She considered going after it but didn't really want to touch it. While she hesitated, a wave enveloped it with foam and rolled it under, out of sight. She thought about it awhile, remembering what Worth had said about low tide exposing old bones, then slowly walked back to where the pillows had been and squatted. Every time a raindrop struck the shingle, a tiny wisp of steam drifted up. She gingerly touched the damp stone surface and found it almost hot.

"There's nothing here, miss. We're ready to go." The grumpy man was standing not ten feet away.

"The shingle's hot," she said. "Look at it steam."

"Probably the same thing that killed the fish," he said. "Your meteoroid. Probably heated up everything."

"Just in spots? Look there and there and—"

"How should I know?"

He looked like he was going to argue with her, then thought better of it. With a little shrug he squatted and felt the stone, obviously just to humor her, but then their glances met. "You're right." He whispered an oath as he pushed himself erect. Then he went to check the beach where fish still lay scattered.

"What is it?" one of the men called from the car, where they were strapping the stretcher on the back.

"Maybe nothing. Maybe not. Let's get her inside."

"Him, you mean."

"Her. We're not responsible for him."

They made her sit beside the driver on the trip back to the house. The other two men sat directly behind her, blocking her view of the stranger. No one said much. She got the impression they didn't want to talk in front of her.

Worth was waiting at the ramp when the car pulled into the service entrance freight dock. She looked grim. She took Merry's arm, ostensibly to help her down, but didn't release her grip until the stranger on the stretcher had been carried away. "You're going straight to the medichek," she announced, leading the way down a side corridor of the basement. "For all you know that person has some dread disease—"

"He's only seasick," Merry protested.

"You don't know that! Do you know what trouble I'll be in if you get sick from this? 'Why did you let her near him?' your parents will ask, and when I say you gave me the slip, they won't accept that! I'll be *out*. Finished!"

"We could all have been killed by the meteoroid," Merry said. "It could have hit the house. Whose fault would that be?"

"I'm talking about your willful carelessness," Worth said, ignoring all else. "Approaching a total stranger! Not once but twice. You said you came here to think and rest! Not to get hurt! In here." She opened a door with a red cross on it. "The clothes go in there to be tested and cleaned." She pointed. "You go in there for a shower, then onto the check bed."

"It's an antique," Merry decided, surveying the unit. It looked like a chaise longue positioned beneath an instrument hood against a wall of dials.

"It still works. Now hurry. They'll want to bring that boy in here as soon as you're finished. I'll wait outside."

Security was tiresome, Merry thought as she slid onto the chaise longue and the hood lowered over her. Security people saw danger where none existed, frightened you of harmless things. Their jobs made them paranoid and also gave them a sense of importance. If there was no danger, of what use were they? Still, two people she knew had been kidnapped, and one was never found.

The breathing mask dropped in place, its rim smooth and cold. "Please inhale. Hold your breath for a count of ten," the medical computer ordered. She obeyed. "Slowly exhale until all the air is out of your lungs. Very good. Please focus on the green dial directly above your face. . . ." The instructions droned on and on. The little room smelled of old leather and the mint-scented water of the shower.

The machine pronounced her healthy. Worth escorted her to her rooms and told her she was to stay there until the beach and grounds had been thoroughly searched. A guard was posted outside her door.

"I might as well be a government prisoner," Merry said bitterly.

"Bite your tongue!" Worth shuddered before she could control the reflex. "I'm going to interview our . . . visitor." She went on rubbing her arms as if she were cold. "You might as well get to your studies."

"Yes," Merry agreed vaguely and shut the door, preoccupied in mulling over Worth's shudder. To qualify for her job Worth was expert in martial arts, marksmanship, and emergency medical care; she could drive or pilot any vehicle, scale a wall, run ten miles, and carry one hundred pounds deadweight down a fifty-foot ladder. What would scare *her*?

Merry sat down at the terminal and tried to study. Math was her weakest subject, and she'd worked on it all summer. Algebra bored her at the best of times; she just didn't care what *y* equaled. Shutting off the sound, she let her thoughts wander over the events of the morning and the night before. What had made the shingle hot? Had the other pillows caught fire when they opened? That foam had smoked as if it were acid. And were there people trapped inside? Had the boy hurt himself falling, as the men thought, or had someone hit him? . . . She kept seeing that burned bone washing against the rocks.

The distant drone of a small boat caught her attention, and she hurried to the bedroom window with the ocean view. Three small craft were out there, cruising slowly back and forth over the water where the glowing thing had disappeared.

"So they do believe me!" she whispered triumphantly. She got her binoculars and settled herself on the window seat to watch the search operation.

Worth woke her at lunchtime. "What did the boats find?" Merry asked, sitting up and rubbing a sleepy seed from one eye. She hadn't heard Worth knock.

"Nothing. A few charred pieces of wreckage. The boy says his small craft crashed in the lightning storm."

"Did they find any of the black pillow things?"

"No . . . that is a bit much." Worth permitted herself a quick smile.

"But it's true!" Merry insisted. "He came out of one—it stank inside, and he did, too. . . ." She saw the look on the woman's face, and her voice trailed off.

"Oh, come now," Worth said, attempting to cajole. "We know you're lonely here. And bored. There's no reason why you shouldn't be. You were satisfied until you got rested up, but it's quite provincial. It's only natural you'd want to stir things up. But the truth is, some spoiled kid old enough to know better got caught in the storm, wrecked his aircar, and was lucky enough to drift ashore, where you found him. It's as simple as that." She turned to leave, saying, "Your lunch is ready. After lunch you can visit him. He wants to thank you for saving his life."

"I didn't save his life."

"He says you did. He's very grateful."

"Did he act funny?"

"People often do when they're in shock."

"He talked like a baby, a little child."

A slight frown crossed the woman's face. "Yes, at first," she admitted, "but then as he came around—you have to remember he's had a big scare. Some people temporarily regress under trauma."

"Does that mean you believe him and not me?"

Worth hesitated. "As I said, your lunch is ready. Oh, you're free now to go anywhere within the house. The grounds are still off limits," Worth concluded.

"Why?" asked Merry.

"Just in case there are more strangers. In any event this boy will be a guest until we can check his story. He says he's from Halifax. He's nineteen—almost twenty—and his name is Mikel Goodman. So far we can't confirm that." Worth made a face. "You would pick a place without phone or radio contact." Then, remembering something else, she laughed sarcastically. "House security had him put in a special room because, and I quote— the stranger may be a commoner and shouldn't see the wealth of the house—"

"I think that's smart," said Merry. "I wouldn't have thought of that. How do you know I'll be safe with him?"

"He's under constant surveillance," Worth said shortly, and left.

chapter IV

HIS ROOM WAS ON THE GROUND FLOOR IN A SECTION OF THE house she'd never been in, through doors and down a gloomy corridor that led eventually to the staff quarters, housekeeping offices, and storeroom, or so the lighted wall plaques said. The room was large and sparsely furnished; its tall windows opened onto a blind courtyard full of wild sunflowers, their heads drooping with age and dampness.

The young man lay stretched out on the bed, his elegant legs crossed at the ankles, his hands clasped behind his head. His hair had dried into soft golden curls. Clad in blue pajamas several sizes too large, he managed to look well-dressed. Even his feet were pretty, she noticed, and was rather astonished by his beauty. The puffy left eye and bruised cheek seemed a desecration.

His whole face lit up when he saw her in the doorway. "It's you!" he said, springing up to welcome her. "I'm so glad . . ." He swayed sideways and abruptly crumpled onto the bed again. ". . . glad to see you . . ." He stared in her direction, his gaze unfocused, blinked several times and closed his eyes. "That's much worse," he decided, and opened them again. "With my eyes shut, I'm still falling, or floating up and down, in and out, rocking. With them open the room goes around, not me." His chuckle was throaty and joyous, making vertigo a joke to be shared with her.

She remained in the doorway, suspicious. His voice and mannerisms were older now, but not much. "You'd better lie down again," she said.

"You're right." He agreed gratefully, as if her idea were so clever he'd never have thought of it himself, and he promptly stretched out again. "Come sit on the bed and talk with me. It'll keep me from thinking how sick I am."

"What's wrong with you?"

"My head hurts, and my stomach, and I can't remember things, and . . ."

As he detailed symptoms, she crossed over to the windows and looked out. Two cardinals were out there in the rain, feeding on fallen sunflower seeds. Sparrows were chirping in the ivy on the opposite wall. By looking up at the windows above, she tried to figure out what part of the house that was, but couldn't, and she listened to the lilting voice behind her.

"How did you get hurt?" she asked. "You weren't when I first saw you."

"I fell." He fingered the swelling. "Do you think it will leave a scar?" he asked, worried.

"I don't know." As she turned, her glance fell on the chandelier's center bulb. It didn't match the rest—a camera lens.

"You see it, too," he said, following her gaze. "They don't trust me. I don't know why. I've been good. What kind of place is this?"

"A country house," she said. "What happened to the pillow— the thing you washed ashore in?"

"It was a life capsule—the latest design." He smiled, exposing perfect teeth. "I sank it. It smelled bad." He looked embarrassed. "You must have noticed that?"

"What happened to the other four capsules?"

He frowned and started to shake his head, then stopped; head-shaking apparently made him dizzy. "I'm sorry," he said. "I don't remember. There were other capsules?"

Merry explained, feeling foolish as she did so, since he listened with complete attention and concern, as if he, too, were humoring her. "They burned, I think," she concluded.

"Burned?" His eyes widened. "What makes you think that?"

"I think—" She paused, hesitant to make such a terrible accusation, yet suddenly sure it was true. "I think you burned them. No one else could have."

He went pale and still, and for long seconds the two stared at each other. "You *think* that?" he whispered in shock. "That's horrible! No wonder I'm being monitored—they must think I'm a monster, a—" He looked from her to the camera, then back to her again, and his expression changed from distress to pity. "You *weren't* lying," he said softly. "You truly believe you saw other capsules, truly believe they were burned, don't you?"

As he spoke, Merry could imagine how this scene might look on a vu-screen. He made her appear the victim of her own imagination, at best—or a liar at worst.

"I saw them," she said firmly. "And so did you."

"I believe you did." He sounded almost angelically sincere. "You truly believe you saw them." His voice faltered, and his eyes filled with tears. "I'm so sorry!"

"That you did it?"

"No! That you could think such a thing! To be so cold and accusing at an age when you should be innocent. To be so distrustful."

It was hard to understand him after that, because he began

to cry. All she could hear clearly was, "I wasn't bad! You mustn't tell these lies!" The rest was garbled sobs and wails. Tears ran down his cheeks, but his gaze never left her face, as if he were gauging her reaction. She didn't understand why he should cry, and so she simply watched, offering no sympathy or comfort. Sobs overwhelmed him; he clenched his fists and twisted on the bed.

There was something familiar about his performance, and after a time she realized it reminded her of scenes from the hoary melodramas stored in the archives of the house computer. In those plays, when a person worked himself up like this, someone always slapped him and he immediately calmed down.

So she tried it, crossing over to the bed and giving him a good quick slap that cracked across his right cheek and made her hand tingle. And it worked, but not quite as she'd expected.

The especially piteous expression he'd assumed as she approached altered to disbelief as she struck; the sobs stopped with an involuntary gasp of surprise. His eyes deepened to green, and as quickly as she'd struck him, he lunged at her. She jumped away. Whatever he was about to do, or try to do, was halted by his fall. For if the hysteria was faked, the vertigo was real. He struggled to get up, fell again, and pounded the floor in frustration—but not crying.

Merry was by this time safely near the door and more than a little frightened by the reaction she'd provoked. In the plays the people slapped always subsided into grateful calm. They never tried to kill you.

"You have to quit lying," she said, determined not to let him know he frightened her, and wondering if anyone was watching on camera or if she was truly alone with him. He rolled over on his back and lay still, his face turned away. In the silence she could hear the cardinals quarreling in the courtyard. "Do you need help getting up?" Not that she was going to risk getting close to him again, but if he said yes, maybe someone would come.

"Have you decided I'm bad, too? You, in that room, watching?" He addressed the camera lens. "Am I evil on your screen?" Carefully pushing himself into a sitting position, he managed to pull himself to the bed and crawl up onto it. "Why do you treat me this way? What have I done? I fall into your sea; I'm alone, sick, and afraid—and all you can do is treat me like a prisoner!" He curled into a ball, his arms embracing his pillow. "I didn't want to come here."

He looked so lonely and miserable she almost felt sorry for him, but instinct warned her not to waste sympathy. Whatever he was, it wasn't what he claimed to be. She was shaking her head as she left the room.

There was no one in the corridor; she had thought Worth might be, but apparently they'd decided he wasn't dangerous. Her father once said that bodyguards were only as good as their imaginations. Merry felt Worth's imagination was lacking.

Why did he keep saying, "I've been good," like a baby expecting punishment?

A short way down the corridor she stopped. She didn't feel like going back to the solitude of her rooms for the rest of the day. What she wanted to do was go to the barn and visit the animals. Animals were very comforting when a person was lonesome and scared. They were glad to see you, and they were warm and furry, and they let you hug and pet them. But the grounds were still off limits. She turned around and surveyed the corridor stretching off into the distance. Since she was here and had nothing else to do, she decided she might as well explore this part of the house.

In all the time she'd been here she hadn't ventured beyond the occupied portion of the building, not because it was forbidden but because it intimidated her, as did the household staff.

The staff, while polite and unfailingly correct, were not friendly, and the girl was always aware that she and Worth were outsiders, intruders in their world. Which was true, of course, since the staff had always lived here and ran the farm and kept the house ready for visits by its absent owners. Merry kept asking herself why she should care if servants found her where she had no reason to be, and she had decided that in part of her mind this was still her great-grandmother's house and she didn't want that lady—or her ghost—to think she was a snoop. So she did care, and until now she had confined her explorations to the barn and sheds and greenhouses.

The corridor angled left at a wide door marked "Storerooms A–D." She slid the door open and peered into the gloom of a hangar-like space that housed everything from ceiling-high racks of canned goods to dishes, glassware, and massive rolls of carpeting and fabrics. Two lift trucks were parked nearby.

"May I help you?" the computer's voice inquired.

She started, then saw the gleam of a camera lens. "Thank you, no. I'm just looking," she said, and closed the door.

From an overhead sign marked "Staff Quarters" onward, the white-walled corridor became serpentine. It also became bright and plush, with thick red carpeting underfoot and discreetly expensive chandeliers overhead. In the center of each curve in the left wall gleamed highly polished double doors of oak with brass fittings. A brass name plate identified the occupant of each apartment by name and position: cook, housekeeper, head gardener, agronomist, veterinarian, house physician, and so forth. If the exterior gave any hint of what lay behind those doors, Merry decided, the staff kept themselves in comfort. The rest of the house was shabby by comparison.

On the right a glass wall opened onto an enclosed garden of twisted pines, sculpture, and carefully raked gravel. A pathway through the pines led to a ramp rising to an archway in a crumbling tower—a far more interesting place to explore, to her way of thinking. She found a sliding panel and stepped out into the garden.

The misty air smelled of pine and peat moss. The gravel crunched satisfactorily underfoot. Behind a border of creeping yew a pool stretched beneath the ramp and rimmed the far garden wall. Large, brightly colored *koi* swam there, silently cruising the perimeters, or nosing the surface to investigate the raindrops. She paused on the ramp to watch the venerable fish and wonder if they minded the limitations of their pool as much as she minded hers.

There must have been people in those other capsules. . . . She saw the black bone floating. How could he set fire to people, even if they were dead? And how did he get something so wet and cold to burn? How could he put the remains in the sea—especially when he could hardly stand up? How crazy did he have to be to do that—or what did he want to hide? A cold raindrop struck her hair and spattered through to her scalp; she shuddered and ran up to the shelter of the arch.

Weeds grew there where sunlight and rain soaked the rubble. Fox grass brushed against her legs as she ducked beneath a chain and pushed open the old-fashioned door at the rear of the arch. The door scraped across a floor deep in sand and plaster dust. The little round room was empty, its ceiling fallen.

Across the room an identical arch opened onto a huge cluttered space. She went in and closed the door. The cluttered space had been a stage, a rather large one. Its curtains were gone, its orchestra pit empty. Beyond, curved rows of seats were draped in dusty tarpaulins. Somewhere in the theater's gloom a rat squeaked. Ornamentation had fallen from a side wall, exposing a rusty beam. The place smelled of rotting fabric, dust, and long disuse. A grand piano stood closed and locked, the thick dust on the lid dotted with lumps of fallen plaster.

You could seat at least two hundred people here, she decided, counting the risers as she climbed toward the lobby, but she couldn't imagine when that many people had come to this house—or who might have sung or acted here. Perhaps the house computer remembered.

From the theater she followed one narrow hall into another, walked ramps and passages, climbed stairs. She found a courtyard herb garden obviously still in use; a pile of cow manure had been dumped in an empty plot. She stepped through an open door and roamed through room after room of empty apartments, some with their own kitchens and service rooms. All were high-ceilinged; many had walls cracked and water-stained from leaky windows or burst pipes. Some rooms were completely empty except for dust balls blowing across the stone or parquet floors; in others headboards from old beds leaned against the walls, mattresses were stacked in corners and inhabited by mice. Antiques the wealthy would have fought for in the city stood here, forgotten; furniture thick with dust, handwoven fabrics molding to ruin, clocks so old some still had liquid crystals, rover units shaped like dogs, their power-paks removed. Mirrors gave back ghostly images as she passed, her footsteps echoing in the stillness.

One suite appeared to have been undisturbed from the time its owner left—how long ago? No furniture was covered; the rugs were still in place. Jewelry and cosmetic jars remained on the counter in the dressing room she entered. Beyond was a bathroom with a clear dome ceiling to give life to the desert garden that filled one side of the room. There was a jagged hole in the dome, but the cacti still stood, mummified, white-needled and pale brown. The sunken blackstone tub was big enough to swim in, and in the sand that had blown into the tub lay what appeared to be an infant's skeleton, half buried. Around it lay tiny lizard and mouse bones and a rope of jade beads strung on a fine gold chain.

She stood staring down at the skeleton and then shook her head. They had to know it was here. It was very old. Whatever had happened, had happened long ago. She hurried out, not touching anything, shaken.

Down the hall from that suite a sign hung from a chain stretched from wall to wall. She stepped over the barrier and read: DANGER! DO NOT ENTER! THIS WING STRUCTURALLY UNSOUND.

If the place collapsed on her, no one would even know. They might guess, of course, when she didn't show up for dinner. The image of herself buried in rubble wasn't all that attractive—especially since she had no idea where she was within the building.

Peering up and down the corridor revealed an area of light. She headed for it and found the corridor ended at an open rotunda. From the railing she looked down three levels onto an empty fountain and up four to see the clouds above a bubble dome. A spiral ramp wound up to the overlook.

After reading that sign, she found the ramp made her nervous, but it seemed firm enough as she climbed, keeping close to the wall. As soon as she could see out the dome, she knew where she was—in the highest tower. The main entrance to the house faced south. There were the mountains, almost lost in fog; the barns and the ocean . . . She stopped and rubbed the grimy glass to see more clearly.

Out where the meteoroid had gone under, a very large ship was anchored, bristling with cranes and other equipment. It was too far away for her to be sure, but it looked like a mining vessel, which meant that other people had recognized the meteoroid and thought it was metal.

She could hardly wait to tell Worth. No one would send a

ship that size to hunt the remains of an aircar.

A flock of crows flew past, cawing raucously, chasing and diving and enjoying themselves, ignoring the mist and rain. She liked crows; they were a rowdy, companionable lot, ready to make the best of things whatever the circumstances.

She returned her attention to finding the shortest way back to the occupied zone of the house. If she followed that el, where pigeons sat in a row along the ridgepole, and turned left into the wing that was only two stories high and had bubble windows, that might lead to the portrait gallery.

Minutes later she was hurrying through the gallery, feeling more secure, when a picture caught her eye. She detoured for a closer look, then stopped, surprised and pleased to find an ancestor here with her own name. *Meredith Elizabeth Allyn Ambrose, b. March 9, 4609—d. July 18, 4733*, said the brass tag on the bottom of the frame. She died six years after I was born, Merry thought, and studied the face. It looked a little like she would if she wore her hair that way, except that this person was much better-looking, tall and casually elegant in a white velvet suit with a short satin cape brushed by a breeze from the balcony behind her. Her right hand held a velvet mask, and her left hand . . . Merry stepped closer. On the woman's left hand was a gold ring with a large green stone. That, too, looked familiar.

But it wasn't until she saw that the portrait was followed by those of her grandparents' and parents' that she realized this was her great-grandmother—as she had looked long before they'd met. With a little thrill of recognition she reached up and shyly touched that painted cheek, wondering at its youth. She sat down cross-legged on the polished floor and stared up at the face that might become her own. She was still there when the house lights came on at five that evening.

chapter V

THERE HAD BEEN A METEOROID, BUT NO ONE ON EARTH had seen it. Not this time. A mass of icy stone and iron, it had traveled an elongated elliptical orbit around the sun and far out past Mars to the asteroid belt, before curving back deep into Earth's orbit. Once the two had nearly met. While Earth remained indifferent, the meteoroid, excited by this contact with an atmosphere, became a meteor, a blazing fireball. It missed Earth by thirty miles and with a sonic boom roared back out into space, its orbit slightly altered. Ten orbits and seven hundred and five years later, it was seen by tracking telescopes in Terra II, The Shepherd Moon.

Because a shepherd moon controls the orbits of other moons, and Terra II governed the other ninety original colonies, it was nicknamed The Shepherd Moon by the media of Earth's Colonial Era. The first colony built, Terra II was the best and most elaborate, designed to sell the advantages of living in space to the crowded areas of Earth. As a product name, The Shepherd Moon was a good sales tool, romantic, yet vague enough to suggest everything from benign authority to a more gentle agrarian past. The reality behind that name was a very different thing.

Now, when their computer warned of a large incoming mass on an orbital collision course with their sister world, Terra IV, those special few inside The Shepherd Moon who received this information said nothing, issued no warning. The telescopes were turned off, the observatories closed; that portion of the computer's voice was stilled. All shuttle service was halted, all view portals sealed, all communication between the worlds temporarily suspended—due to solar storms, they said.

There was no point in causing panic. Their data indicated that there was neither room enough nor water enough for the other worlds to take in the people from Terra IV. They could not be fed or housed, their waste and dead converted. To take them in would result in chaos and possible questioning of authority. It would mean endless work and inconvenience and petty decisions—all tiresome. On such short notice it was futile to think of sending people to the old world—Earth. No one would want to go, and there was no time to re-educate them. It was common knowledge that their ancestors had built the Terra worlds when Earth became overcrowded and barbaric. The data banks were vague as to how Earth's people became enemies; there was reference to a chaotic period in the distant past, but details had long since been eroded away by time. Besides, there were no shuttles capable of such a trip and no time in which to build them. No one would suffer.

With exquisite detachment Terra II's scientist-rulers agreed that, since they could do nothing to stop the meteoroid, silence was the kindest course. After all, they reassured one another, many worlds had died. They no longer knew how many. Some had been vacant for centuries, emptied by disease or fungus, before their untended shells imploded and their atmospheres froze in space. In time The Shepherd Moon might die—they hoped not in their time, of course. The best they could do now was to secretly expel a few special research capsules and hope the forces of disaster would carry them to Earth. If anyone survived the trip, there might be a possibility of future migration. They hoped that this decision, painful as it was, would assure any who might question their handling of the incident of their sensitivity. But they expected no one to question their authority.

The meteoroid hit Terra IV like a bullet through an egg. The side of the shell struck first imploded into fragments that flashed fire before the balance of the shell crushed inward. No screams, no sound at all could be heard. For a second what had been a hollow sphere became a ragged metal bowl, and then the bowl was punctured and slowly tore apart. Within a period of two minutes, seven million people died, their bodies turned to freeze-dried husks floating in the black vacuum of space.

The meteoroid pushed the wreckage into a new orbit before breaking through and hurtling on. Larger chunks of debris trailed along the meteoroid's new route, eventually to be pulled with it into the sun. A piece of Terra IV's outer hull, looking now like crushed tinfoil, went tumbling off toward Earth, caught by her gravity. The fall took almost two days. Merry witnessed its ending.

As the debris' orbit decayed, human and other particles pulled along in its gravity wake began to glow in the atmosphere and quickly gasified. The debris flared and by burning lost mass and slowed. Research capsules behind it were consumed by its fiery tail, but one tumbled wide to fall charred but intact into the ocean.

The observers in The Shepherd Moon heard five reassuring signals. Five cadets of the original one hundred had reached Earth's surface alive. When four signals ceased abruptly six hours later, eyebrows were raised. Hope and interest in possible migration faded. It had been just a thought, impractical at best. The smaller the world, the greater the world-weariness.

How degrading to be watched, deprived of privacy, forced to be aware of every move one made because one might be judged by it. He regarded the lens in the chandelier; it could be fused, but that would gain nothing but self-betrayal. They'd replace it and watch him more closely.

Fire was a wonderful thing, primitive, exciting—if not very efficient. Things didn't burn completely. He'd never been allowed to use this energy before, never dared to break *that* rule. He knew why when he saw them ignite. Did all things smell so ghastly when they flamed, so raw and unsophisticated?

How odd that of them all a child should cause him fear. She thought he'd burned them, she'd said, which meant she wasn't sure. But she had known his grief wasn't real. They looked to be a loutish lot, as he'd been taught, but they weren't stupid— which was a shame since he'd counted on that.

If only he hadn't lost faith, hadn't been numbed by despair before the capsule opened. But the fear of being trapped in there, of dying in that stinking wet darkness . . .

How strange to have his mind free. Odd memories and images broke loose and floated to the surface. He remembered being a baby, floating in the tank, feeling sounds pulse through the liquid and his body. Not until he was lifted out, tied off and dried, and taken to the nursery did he understand that he was separate from the tank. It wasn't part of him. He remembered crying, wanting to go back. The mamatrons were warm and safe and cuddling, but he never trusted them after understanding he was a separate, vulnerable thing that could be picked up and taken from them without warning.

He was a product of genetic engineering—but then all his people were. There was no time or room for nonspecific types, for random variants. His world had become as carefully structured as living cells and as totalitarian.

After three months in the tank, when he was still more head than human, the music had begun pulsating through his liquid entity, imprinting, altering, programming measurements of time into his forming brain. He could hear it always, a background noise as lulling as the sea. And he could sing it, all of it, from beginning to end. He had forgotten the tank until he entered the capsule and it was filled and sealed and he felt the sounds and then the cold silence of space. Had the Master known he would remember?

Visual training began in the nursery. Before he learned to walk and talk, he could see the colors radiated by each living thing, that pale cloud of electrons that surrounds them. He was taught to recognize their condition by the color and intensity of that radiation, a task so simple that soon only the abnormal held his interest. He found it interesting, for example, that illness and anger were often the same color, and either condition, when prolonged, faded into the other. Holding out his right hand, he saw he was now radiating a cold pale green instead of his normal golden yellow. He sighed and let his hand slip.

These people *touched* him! They didn't even hesitate but put their hands on his body! He was never touched as a baby, not by humans. Only by the mamatrons. But he was talked to, constantly fed information in one form or another. He was exercised and nourished but never touched. None of his group was. They were too special. "Touch alters comprehension," the Master said. "Touch confuses. With touch the mind seeks meaning where there is none."

It was an honor to be chosen. Of all the honors the Master could confer, being chosen for this mission was the greatest. So the Master said. Mikel had controlled his doubt, not allowing it to show as he studied and memorized all he had to learn. Cadets were not permitted doubts. Doubt caused confusion, and confusion could be fatal. But why was he the only Life Cadet chosen, and the other ninety-nine of lower rank?

He was born and trained to serve and did so. By the age of five he could see a laboratory mouse emitting radiation that signaled malfunctioning cells, hold his hands above the mouse, and by his own energy correct the problem. At twelve he could induce healing in a broken bone. It was often very simple, taking only seconds. Some bad cells died of cold or heat—usually of heat. All he had to do was induce fever until the color changed, then lower the temperature back to normal. Virus required more energy than bacteria. For the most resistant fungi the carrier was often completely purified to keep the spores from spreading. The aged were also purified. Purifications were always done in private, the gas recycled, the ash disposed of.

There were the Throwbacks who resented his type, who would have killed him if they could. They tried in subtle, sneaky ways, ignorant of some of his talents. He was bred and trained to feel no emotion. The imperfections to be eradicated in the body concerned a Life Cadet, not the personality the body housed. Sometimes he was tempted to violate that rule, to try to feel— but that was bad. When he was bad, he was punished. But when he was good and walked his shifts in shining yellow and people sought him out and smiled to see his beauty . . . he could have become a Master. No! That was a bad thought . . . think good. Masters got old. He would never age.

He could sing and make these people respond to him—but that might betray him. He wasn't ready yet.

This space was so much bigger than his quarters at home, but it was so drab—no yellows, no pastels that were not gray-toned.

On the beach there had been flying things that made shrill sounds. He wanted to ask what they were but couldn't. He might be expected to know. Those growing things outside the window were bedraggled by the rain. But then the rain itself was bedraggled here, cold and gray and endless. In Terra II the rain was never cold, and the water was always a pastel shade. It lasted fifteen minutes, quite long enough to appreciate color, tone, and texture, but not long enough to bore. He turned his back on the window. He'd never see Terra II again. Why didn't they stop the rain?

He shifted restlessly, anxious. What was he supposed to do here? Lexus shouldn't have screamed and fought. It was so unfair of him. They couldn't all be found together—Lexus should have understood that. One stranger could be explained, accepted, but five would be a threat. Not only did he outrank the other four, but he had come out first and was entitled. Survive, the Master said, for someday we may join you.

They spoke of a meteoroid, those louts who handled him so roughly. They thought a meteoroid had fallen into their ocean, that its coming had created a freak storm that had brought him down. They had given him his story through their speculations, those coarse men who thought they were so clever but never guessed that he was conscious all the time, that he permitted those indignities they inflicted on him. He could have killed them . . . but then he might have died of cold.

He smiled at the idea that he had let them live in exchange for their blanket and shelter. As soon as he was acclimated to this uncivilized world—where they lacked even the knowledge to keep the outdoors at a comfortable temperature—as soon as he was able, he would even the score with those men.

In the room next door an aged physician watched a monitor screen and wondered. The subject repeatedly thrashed about on the bed, then curled into fetal position, hugging arms to chest. He was running a slight fever, and his actions hinted of possible pain, yet the scanners had shown no injury aside from the facial cuts and abrasions. The rapid pulse and respiration could be due to trauma, reaction to the immunization, the prolonged vertigo to inner ear disturbance from wave motion, or all three. The physician could have accepted all that except for the clothes he had arrived in and his brain wave readout. The former would attract too much attention if worn outside his quarters; the latter was similarly foreign.

The jumpsuit perhaps could be dismissed. She had been assigned to this house for fifteen years (by choice; her security clearance was total), and in that time styles and fabrics changed with the ruling class. In her uniformed world fashion had little importance. It was possible that the yellow suit was the latest style among Halifax socialites—if he was a member of that class. She doubted that, just as she doubted he was sane, but she had no proof of her suspicions. The computer labeled his analysis within normal range, but had given him wide-spectrum immunization and had labeled his voice print: "Not valid. Retest at normal respiration rate. Regional accent: unknown. Acquired accent: Ubiquitous Media."

Where had he been born that he had missed immunization in infancy? In her long career she had seen many eccentricities among the ruling class, aversions to certain sensible rules and regulations. Some families thought themselves above the rules; others genuinely feared ingesting any product mass-produced, suspecting contamination or resultant retardation. Which thought reminded her of another oddity about this patient: he gave his age as twenty-one and was of a size to be, but hadn't yet reached puberty, apparently due to endocrine manipulation. She knew of no reproduction programs so severe, even among the most retarded classes. Who had done this to him?

In a few days when he felt better and his vertigo had passed, she was going to administer more tests and ask questions. For now, the important thing was rest and nourishment. So far he had refused all food, revolted by its sight and smell. The meat particularly seemed to disgust him, as did the glass of milk.

The thought occurred to her as she watched him that he wasn't used to this atmosphere. She had been a diver in her youth, fascinated by the underwater ruins of the past, and on deep dives, as the air mix in the tanks changed to accommodate increasing pressure, one's mental outlook, as well as the pitch of one's voice, changed with the air supply. Some of his reactions reminded her of that—but in his case that made no sense.

He was staring at the camera again, that same odd smile lighting his face, as if he knew a secret that pleased him very much. He was such a handsome boy, quite beautiful. His people must be frantic with worry. If he had people? He hadn't asked to call anyone. Perhaps he had escaped from a private mental hospital? That might account for the bright clothing, to identify him instantly if he left the grounds. And if the girl's story was accurate . . . He had nearly attacked her—but then she'd had no right to slap him.

She got up and poured herself a cup of coffee and stood lost in thought. With any luck they would find the flotation gear he'd sunk. That might answer some questions. Taking her coffee back to the monitor desk, she smiled to herself. Whatever his story turned out to be, as a patient he was interesting, a welcome change from the routine of minor cuts and animal bites that were her usual work . . . why couldn't the poor boy sleep?

chapter VI

THREE DAYS PASSED. THE RAIN AND FOG CONTINUED. NO more strangers were found, or any trace of wreckage. The house, never lively, became even more hushed, as if it, too, were depressed by the gloom.

Merry spent most of her time curled up on a library window seat that overlooked the lawns and sea. She didn't know what to do with herself. Not just now, in this waiting period, but *always*, for that was how she defined her future. She didn't want to be like her parents—although they were no different from the parents of her friends. They all said, "I'm so busy!" And they were—or at least their time was taken up. But what they did most of, she realized as she watched the rain, was what she had done all summer—nothing. And she knew she couldn't stand a lifetime of that.

The hard part was deciding what to become. There were so many things she wanted to study: music, insects, zoology, ancient literature, agriculture—but to what end? She couldn't always be a student, and to study everything meant to excel in nothing. In the cellar library vaults she'd found a book on Leonardo da Vinci, and he had written of himself, "As every divided kingdom falls, so every mind divided between many studies confounds and saps itself." He had seldom finished anything he started, and he was a genius, which she wasn't. Whatever she decided on, she wanted to be the best. But her ultimate goal remained as unclear as the weather.

Every now and then the fog would lift long enough to show the ship still at anchor where the meteoroid went down. At night sometimes ship's lights made glowing dots through the mist. But no matter how often she checked with her binoculars, she didn't see them recovering anything.

Never before had she had so much free time, and never before had she been so lonesome. She'd enjoyed the summer, when solitude was her choice, but from the week her parents were to return and did not, she'd been ready to go home. In her darkest moods now she worried that they had met with an accident and people could not bring themselves to tell her. Then she would convince herself that idea was silly, that any day now an aircar would arrive. But none did. The rain seemed to wash hope away, little by little, leaf by leaf. Studying, reading, practicing the piano, watching old dramas, she was aware of being alone.

Mealtimes were the worst. No matter how hungry she was, food tended to lack flavor after the first few bites. In the carpeted and wood-paneled stillness of the dining room, with Williams, the butler, hovering somewhere behind her, she was aware of every noise her silver made against her plate. Rolls broke with startling crispness and crumb showers. At a table meant for twenty, hers was the only place setting.

At home she ate with friends in the penthouse dining room. From their table in the Minors Alcove she could look across the big room to where her parents often dined with her friends' parents. In a room seating two hundred, she knew every name.

While a few of the building's owners kept kitchens and staff, most preferred to use the common facilities because, they said, "Less staff, less aggravation." From the windows of that penthouse dining room these privileged few could look out across the lights of the city to the mountains, and eat and talk and laugh, as secure as if they owned the world—as in a sense they did—or all of it that mattered.

"Why don't you visit Mikel?" Worth suggested, seeing her spending her afternoon on the window seat for the third day in a row.

"Mikel?" Merry asked, surprised by such familiar reference to the stranger.

"The boy you rescued. He's charming company now that he's feeling better." Worth missed the nuance of tone and went on, warming to her subject. "We've been telling him about our childhoods, the staff and I. His questions made us remember things we'd forgotten years ago." Her voice trailed away in reflection; her face darkened and tightened. "How we were fed, how we were told we were orphans, the dormitories at night." Old rage smoldered in her eyes, and then the bland, impersonal mask of the good servant reappeared. Her tone implied total indifference as she concluded. "I just thought you might find him interesting, since he's of your class."

"I don't like him," Merry said, uneasy in her ignorance of the cause of Worth's anger; she knew nothing of the woman's past and had been taught it was extremely rude to ask personal questions of the staff.

"Whatever you say."

"I think he's dangerous."

Worth's lips tightened in a narrow smile. "I wouldn't allow you near him if I thought that. Are you saying I don't know my job?"

"You don't know him—only what he's told you." Merry

was determined not to be intimidated by her.

"And you, with your years of experience, you know better?"

"I know he's not what he says he is," Merry said quietly, her eyes never leaving Worth's. "He's acting."

"As you wish." Worth turned to go, and as a parting shot added, "You're as paranoid as the medic here. She's afraid of him, too."

Merry wanted to call after her, "I'm not afraid of him!" but didn't. To do so would be undignified as well as untrue. Maybe she was paranoid. People said you couldn't live in a city without getting that way—afraid of every stranger. If she hadn't seen the beach that morning, had met the boy only after he was brought in, as Worth had, would that have made a difference?

Distracted by the sight of an aircar emerging from the clouds, she leaned closer to the rain-spotted window. With the gloomy light she couldn't be sure, but the car was large and dark. She grabbed her binoculars, but by that time the car had passed on over the house. The rain fell in streaks, shaken from the clouds by the craft's current. Then above the rain she heard the car circling, coming back, its airfoils whining as it came in to land.

It was her parents! It had to be! They were the only people who knew where she was. She set off at a run, worried that their pilot might not see the water on the landing pad and skid and disable the car so they couldn't leave right away. Someone, a man's voice, shouted, "Wait!" as she ran across the main lobby. People were coming at a run from both sides of the corridor. She heard Worth call, "Don't go out there," from the mezzanine above, but ignored her.

The pilot had set down, not on the landing pad, but where the gravel driveway widened near the barns. One glance told her she was right; the gold seal gleamed against the car's wine-red finish. They'd borrowed one of Grandfather's state cars to come back to get her.

Minus coat, hat, and boots, she ran out into the rain, down the wide terrace steps and over to the flagstone path along the avenue of pines. Puddles flew with every footfall. Seeing her run, the dogs began to bark excitedly. The aircar's hatch slid open, the ramp eased down. A man in the uniform of a State Security Forces captain stepped out, holding a large umbrella for the man who followed.

He's gained weight, Merry thought, catching a glimpse of the second man silhouetted against the glow of the cabin lights. "Hello, Father," she called happily. She was out of breath from running and had to wipe water from her eyes. Both men glanced around, startled, peering down at her from the shelter of the black umbrella. Only then did she realize her mistake. "Grandfather!" Something must be wrong and he'd come to tell her.

Her grandfather returned her stare, then, recovering himself, muttered something to his aide, took the umbrella, and came down the ramp. In his burgundy-red uniform he looked like the luxury model of his son, older, more powerful, with thicker upholstery and gold trim. His curly salt-and-pepper hair, close cut, shone even in this light, as did his beard, which had gone almost completely white. The beard, carefully styled to conceal a too-aggressive jaw, rounded and refined his image, which at first glance appeared benign.

"Let's go along to the house, shall we?" He spoke as if they met like this every day. "The old place looks the same. Still beautiful, even in the rain." His warm, dry, carefully manicured hand closed over her cold, wet paw, and she was easily turned and aimed back along the flagstones, then set free to walk beside him. "I've always loved the air here," he confided, "the mixed scents of pine and hardwood and sea." He interrupted himself to advise an approaching servant, "A party of three, Vincent. We'll be staying the night, perhaps longer," then asked her, "Do the wild geese still stop on their way south?"

"Yes," she said, surprised out of her shock. "There were some this morning."

"Ah." He nodded, pleased. "Perhaps I'll get to see them. And the deer. Do they still come down out of the woods at dawn?"

"I don't know. My rooms face the ocean—"

"Then you'd see them only if you were outside and very quiet." There was a slight hesitation in his step as they passed Worth at the bottom of the terrace. "Your bodyguard?"

"Yes."

"Ah. You've been here all this time. All summer?"

"Yes." She looked up at him, but his attention was on the steps, which were slippery with wet maple and sycamore leaves. He handed the umbrella, still open, to Williams at the door. "We'll be in the library, Williams. We'll want brandy, hot tea, and a blanket. See that we're not disturbed. Oh, the two men with me are aides, not guests. Quarter them accordingly. They'll dine with staff. And have these steps cleared and kept that way."

"Of course, sir. It's good to see you again, sir." Williams closed the umbrella with a flourish and hurried off as if glad to have a purpose. Merry couldn't help noticing the staff's deferential attitude, a very different one from the casual service she was given. She also noted that somewhere they had found bright red service jackets and wore them.

"When were you last here?" she asked as they crossed the lobby, making conversation for the benefit of listeners, outsiders, as all staff people were.

"Seven years ago."

"How do you remember names?"

"I was born here. I knew Vincent when he was four and I was six. Williams' mother was our vegetable gardener. Vincent's father was the day chef. He may still be, come to think of it."

He allowed her to precede him into the library and, as the door slid shut behind them, stood looking at the beautiful room.

It was copied from a famous thirtieth-century library. The murals on its softly curving panels had been painted by Houbegun of Albany. There were secluded viewing screens and cave-like alcoves leading to the book vaults. In a recessed bay opposite the windows, logs burned in an enclosed fireplace, and soft chairs beckoned.

"Ah. I see the window seat is your favorite place to look out on the world. It was mine." He walked over, picked up the binoculars, and stood musing. "When I was your age, I would sit in here on days like this and wonder if I would be trapped here always, away from all that mattered. I was sure that somewhere, beyond my boundaries, there were fascinating people whose sophistication would rub off on me, whose smallest conversation sparkled with wit and charm, people among whom I would find a friend. And I actually found two, which isn't bad." He fell silent for a moment; a wry smile twitched the corner of his mouth before he put the binoculars down and turned to find her watching him. She was curled up in one of the rose-colored chairs by the fireplace, shoes off, feet tucked beneath her. "May I ask *why* you are here?"

She told him and then could wait no longer. "Are my parents all right?"

"They're quite well. I spoke with your father last week. They're staying at a villa in the Georgian Islands. Some newfound friends. Your father was excited about a Five Moon Party he was giving . . ."

"He loves parties," she said lamely, torn between relief and anger.

"Yes."

There was an awkward silence, and then she said, "They forgot I was here."

"It would appear so," the general said quietly. "I'm sorry. Had I known—"

"It's not your fault. I shouldn't have come. They said it wasn't normal."

"Did they?" A strange expression crossed his face, and his eyes narrowed.

A discreet two-tone chime announced the entrance of Williams pushing a tea cart. Not for this house the impersonal efficiency of robo-servers. On the top shelf of the cart were tea, a decanter, and glasses; on the lower a beige cashmere blanket and fleece booties.

While the general chatted with Williams, inquiring after the butler's family and other local people, she put on the pair of booties and covered up with the blanket. Her feet were wet and she was cold with anger, rain, and nerves. This whole scene felt unreal, as if she'd somehow blundered into one of her dumber dreams. They had *forgotten*—or were they subtly punishing her for going against their wishes?

"I don't know your mother," August Ambrose began as the door closed behind Williams. "We've been acquainted only fifteen years. We've never had occasion to get beyond small talk. I do know your father. There's less to him than meets the eye."

"Do you think you should say things like that to me about them?" she asked, loyal in spite of her current feelings.

"Perhaps not, but you're at that age when one can be devoured by self-doubt. When what one feels or wants—or wants to be—can be so easily ridiculed by others. And one's life is altered permanently, usually not for the better. Some feelings of inferiority at thirteen are justified, of course, but not yours. Not where that pair's concerned."

He reached over and handed her the tea, picked up his drink, sipped it, and sat back, boots stretched toward the fire. Raindrops still beaded the softly glowing leather. Taking a napkin, he polished the spots away. The ruby ring he always wore flashed fire as his hand moved.

"Your father never liked me," he said, sitting back again. He chuckled to himself, as if genuinely amused, remembering. "As a boy, Alex used to preface remarks with the phrase 'when Father dies,' instead of the usual 'when I grow up.' He's more discreet now." He looked up from his glass, met her troubled eyes, and sighed. "Forgive me—I'm straying from the point I wished to make. Which is: Never be less than you are. Never lower your standards to please others. Those who would require it aren't worthy of you. Even if they're family. Or perhaps especially."

He finished his drink in one neat swallow and poured another. "Now why don't we discuss something pleasant?"

She was more than ready to. His opinion of her parents might be justified, but she didn't want to hear too much more of it.

"Did you come here for a vacation?"

"No . . . ah . . . on impulse. Just for the night. I was in the area." He gestured toward the window. "The salvage vessel out there. They're in the process of leaving now."

"Did they find anything?"

He shrugged, then gave her an appraising glance. "Do you know what they were hunting?"

"The meteoroid. I saw it fall."

"Did you?" He brightened as if she'd just given him a wanted gift. "Tell me what you saw. Start at the beginning and leave nothing out."

Within minutes both her chill and her anger faded as they discussed a topic both found interesting. He treated her as an equal in both experience and intellect, and when she spoke, he was an attentive listener. Without being aware of it, she went from being miserable to being more content than she had been in months.

Outside, an early evening fell, the clouds darkening with still more rain. The household staff went about their chores as always, but with more effort tonight. Hurried trips were made to the hothouses for prime vegetables. Wines, cheese, and mushrooms were brought up from their respective cellars; grapes and apples chosen for their bloom and perfection; fish filleted and put to chill; lamb saddles marinated. The master suite upstairs, always kept in readiness, was given a final extra polish and smelled of lemon oil and wax.

The pair in the library talked on, like friends long separated and now unexpectedly reunited. In all her years she'd never had the chance to talk with him without fear of interruption. As military governor, he never had the time, moving in the midst of officials, aides, family, guests, and ever-present guards. Now their conversation went from meteors to tektites to music to dogs. He learned she played the piano; she learned he played the flute. She had his undivided attention for more than two hours, and never once in that time did she get the feeling she was boring him or that he didn't believe her.

"We'd better change for dinner," he said then, glancing at his watch. It was a very precious watch, in antique style, with a three-inch-wide gold bracelet and an oval ruby face. Some might have called it vulgar. "You'll dine with me, I hope? We seldom have the chance to talk, and I'm enjoying it so much."

For the first time in months she looked forward to eating in that dining room. She wasn't disappointed; dinner was delicious, and their conversation went on as effortlessly as before. They were interrupted only once when the general called for his aides and asked them to check the young crash victim's story. "Get his tape from the medical computer. Check his ID with Central Registry. You'll have to use the aircar's unit. There's none here. Easthaven was built as a total retreat. I want a full report by ten tonight," he said, dismissing them.

When they'd gone, he entertained her with stories of his boyhood here, seemingly a time of sylvan peace and hunts for offshore treasures and rainy days spent wandering through the deserted wings of the house, as she had that day. "I once counted two hundred and sixty-one rooms," he said. "That doesn't include the cellars and storage vaults. A person could get lost down there and never be found again."

That reminded her, and she told him of the skeleton in the bottom of the tub. His face went blank and paled, as if the story shocked him. His eyes narrowed and searched hers so intently that she felt a twinge of fear. Had she said something terrible? But then he smiled and shook his head ruefully, as if remembering. "Ah," he said, "my little chimpanzee. It's been found at last. It ran away, poor thing. I hunted for it everywhere. I was quite upset at the time."

"What was its name?"

He didn't remember. She tried to picture him at her age and found it difficult. If you were so fond of a pet, how could you forget its name?

"I'd like it very much if you played the piano for me," he said, changing the subject.

It wasn't until after she'd gone to bed that she remembered he'd forgotten to tell her what the salvage ship had found that had brought him here to see it. She would ask him in the morning.

chapter VII

SOMETIME IN THE NIGHT SHE WAKENED, HEART POUNDING as if she'd had a nightmare, but she hadn't. Winds buffeted the house. Gusts slapped rain against the windows. In the bathroom an airshaft made woofling noises in the walls from wind blowing across the mouths of vent stacks on the roof. Water gurgled in spouts, filling cisterns deep beneath the cellars. In each lull came the sound of heavy surf.

Wanting reassurance of safety from the storm before falling back to sleep, she opened one eye and surveyed the room. Nothing was out of place. She was used to city lights, and the darkness of rural nights still made her uneasy. She always left a lamp on in the lounge and the bedroom door open. The muscles of her left arm ached from being slept on. With a deep, sighing breath she stretched and rolled over to see what time it was. Her feet rammed against something solid, and she came wide-awake. Someone was sitting on her bed!

Almost in one move she touched the light switch, slid up into sitting position, as far as she could get from him, and pulled the covers up around her. As she blinked against the light, she saw Mikel sitting there watching her. His cuts and bruises were all healed; he was as physically perfect as when she'd first seen him. More oddly, he was dressed in the gray-and-black uniform of the State Security Forces. The uniform was much too large. If a camera constantly monitored him and he was watched by guards, how had he gotten here? And where did he get the captain's uniform? Then she remembered locking the double doors in the corridor and the side door into the hall, as always, since she didn't like servants walking in on her without knocking.

"How did you get in here? What do you want?"

When he still didn't speak, she reached for the intercom. Swiftly as a striking snake he lunged forward and hit her wrist, throwing her arm back so hard her hand cracked against the padded headboard. He sank back into his original position, legs folded yoga style. She flexed her fingers to make sure nothing was broken.

"Worth says you think I lied." There was a chilling warning in the softness of his voice. "Because of you, two men in these uniforms came to my room. The gold letters on the collar spell SSF! Did you notice?" He smiled and pointed to his collar. "Twice, once on each side—SSF! SSF! Like an animal sniffing— SSF! They were sniffing for the truth, like you. They were going to hurt me."

"Why are you wearing that?" she asked. She was badly frightened, but she wasn't going to let him know.

"Worth said I should, that it would make things easier."

"Worth?"

"She's my friend. She's waiting for me now."

"Worth knows you're *here*?" Something was very wrong.

He nodded. "She told me where to find you." He glanced away, distracted. "I've never had an old and ugly friend before.

I hope she can be trusted. But then she's no uglier than the rest of you."

Merry considered the source and let the insult pass. "If Worth betrayed me, why wouldn't she betray you?" she suggested, hoping to shake him.

His eyes focused on her again. "Do you think she would?"

"Do you?" she asked, and wondered if she could flip the covers back over his head, push him off the bed, and get away before he could untangle himself. Maybe Worth was outside, listening in the lounge? How had he forced her to allow him here? Then she remembered the woman's expression the day before when she spoke of her own childhood. Anger—or hate?

The boy was nodding to himself. "That *is* true. I shouldn't trust her. She might be using me for reasons of her own. As I am using her." He laughed, a delighted little giggle, then sobered. "Worth said to bring you with us as a hostage. But I won't. I'm tired of being told what to do. I'm tired of being good. They can't punish me here."

"Where are you going?" she asked. But instead of answering, he unfolded his legs and got up with a dancer's swift grace. The vertigo was obviously gone.

"Are you afraid of me?" he asked.

"No!" she lied, thinking he was dangerously insane.

"Oh." Disappointed, he glanced around the room, then stepped over to a tubbed plant near the window. "Watch me." The plant was a white camellia, large and profusely blooming, brought in from the hothouse a day or so before. He touched a leaf as if feeling its texture, then stretched out both arms, fingers splayed, hands directly opposite each other. He seemed to caress the air around and over the plant but did not touch the leaves or flowers.

The plant made a rustling sound, and the leaves began to curl. The waxy white flowers turned brown. An herbal scent suffused the room. Then, to Merry's open-mouthed surprise, what looked like a cobalt-blue corona outlined the plant. Not until she saw wisps of carbon did she realize the camellia was burning, and by that time it was incinerated, falling into the pot and onto the red rug as fragile black ashes that curled and melted away. Only the base of the woody stalk remained, a blackened stick protruding from the white gravel covering the potting soil in the tub.

"That's what you did!" she whispered, horrified. "Those things on the beach—not all the bones burned."

"It was wet," he said defensively, as if she'd accused him of doing a sloppy job, "cold and wet. And I was sick and out of phase." He changed the subject. "Are you afraid of me now?"

"You did burn them! But how?"

"You have to be born with the talent." He approached the bed. "You have to be a very special person."

"How could you do that to anyone?"

"You excite the molecules. Make them dance. Then rebond them—or set them free." He smiled, pleased by her interest, pretending she was questioning the mechanics and not the morals of his act. "You can do it with anything, once you practice. Some things excite so easily they're no fun at all." To demonstrate, he held his hand palm down over the intercom. The unit began to sweat beads of liquid and then collapsed into a lumpy puddle.

She looked from the evil-smelling plastic mess on the bedside table to his perfect face. *"What are you?"* The three words were distinct with loathing.

"I was sent from Terra II. I'm going to rule Earth. Worth said I could." He said this without a trace of humor. "She's going to help me learn all the things I must. She said I'm needed here."

"You're crazy!" Merry was trying to remember if Teratu was in Asia or the South Pacific.

"That's what Worth thought at first. But that's because you're ignorant. You think they're all moons, and they're not. Earth built them. Long ago." He paused, distracted by a thought. "Worth said I shouldn't tell anyone. Someone might shoot me. But I can tell you. You won't have time to repeat it. No one else will know until we're ready."

She slid out of bed then, on the side opposite him. He moved to block her route to the door.

"What are you doing?"

"Opening the window. It stinks in here."

"You're trying to get away." The idea seemed to please him. "You *are* afraid."

"Worth said you weren't to hurt me." She was guessing.

"Yes. But she doesn't understand the situation. You'll talk. I have to kill you."

"No one will believe your story." Her voice was casual, but her hands were shaking so that she could hardly release the window catch. When the panel slid open, cold wet wind rushed in. "If I told anyone, they'd think I was crazy, too."

As he came toward her, she recognized the expression on his face; that was how the barn cats looked before they pounced on sparrows. She swung up and out the window onto the narrow, railed track the window cleaner traveled. Wind tugged at her. Soaked leaves clung to the rails and moved beneath her feet. The drop was twenty feet onto a hedge below. If she had to, falling was far preferable to burning. Flattening herself against the wall, she tried to dig her fingers into worn spots and inched toward the next window. Before she got there, the panel slid open and he leaned out, squinting against the rain.

She tried a desperate left side kick, hoping to hit him in the face, but failed and nearly fell. The wind whipped her hair across her eyes and plastered it there, wet, blurring half her view.

Catching a glimpse of his bright head withdrawing, she pressed her cheek against the wall, hoping against hope he'd given up. The metal rail was painfully cold to her bare feet. Her rain-

soaked nightshirt clung and chilled. Leaves her shuffling had
bulldozed scratched and itched around her ankles. A hand appeared, clasping the window frame, a dark boot stepped onto
the sill, and he was standing in the window, reaching out to grab
her left wrist and pull her in. Then suddenly he disappeared, so
quickly that she thought he'd slipped and fallen to the floor—
and hoped he had.

"Get in here!" Worth was at the window, her frizzy hair blowing wildly. "Are you crazy? I'm responsible for you!"

"He wants to kill me!"

"Don't be silly! That's just a trick he plays with a hidden gun."
When the girl didn't respond, Worth warned, "Don't make me
come out there and get you."

Cold minutes passed while the two watched each other. Finally
Worth stepped up on the window sill. As she put her foot down
on the rail, leaves slipped beneath her boot, the rail shuddered
and made a cracking noise as if it were about to pull out of the
wall. With a little cry of fear the woman twisted back, throwing
her weight against the window frame, and managed to fall backward into the room. The rail creaked again, and quivered.

Merry considered shouting for help, then decided not to.
Chances were no one could hear in this wind—except Worth,
who might shoot her to shut her up. She heard them at the other
window then—their voices, not their words. Worth sounded
angry, and the boy as childish as he'd been on the beach that
day. Managing to turn her head, Merry could see them looking
out, but neither attempted to come after her. After a few moments they withdrew and shut the window.

They're probably cold, she thought dimly, hearing the other
window close, and they want to warm up while they decide what
to do. Five minutes passed before she guessed they had solved
their problem by simply locking her out. Even when she had
worked her way close enough to peek around the window frame,

it took some time for her to risk doing so for fear of being tricked and grabbed.

The bedroom was empty. Thinking they might be hiding in the other rooms, she waited to see if they would show themselves, but she was so cold now that her shaking made the railing quake.

The windows were both latched. Desperate, she inched her way around the wall to the bathroom window and found it open just far enough for her to nudge it back with numb fingertips. Hours seemed to pass as she clung out there, shoving on that frame, afraid at any moment she'd slip and fall into the hedge below. When the panel finally opened far enough to be shouldered back, she crawled in headfirst, scraping her stomach on the sill as she slid the last few feet onto the rug.

She lay huddled up for minutes, shaking with nerves and cold, breathing so hard that she whimpered and had to bite her hand to control the sound. After what seemed a long time, she reached up and pulled a towel down and began to dry herself. There wasn't a sound in the outer rooms. She decided the pair had gone—for now, anyway—which was a relief. Her fingers were raw and tender, as were her knees, abraded by the stucco. Her feet were black with wet, oily dust. She wiped them on the towel and felt vaguely wicked doing so, then giggled; a ruined towel was the least thing she had to worry about.

The sound of the aircar lifting off roused her from stupor. She pulled herself up to the open window and blinked against the rain. Too late; the car was gone. Not even its running lights were visible. She sank back against the frame, totally depressed.

The clouds were high and moving fast, backlighted by the moons. Clear sky showed through a break; a star gleamed briefly and was lost again. A man's hoarse shout made her look down. A light bobbed along the driveway. An answering shout came from the barn. Lights she'd never seen before came on, illuminating the grounds and casting long shadows. Something was obviously happening, and standing here being scared didn't do any good.

She dressed hurriedly in sweater and slacks, stepped barefoot into beach shoes, and set off. She had barely touched the brass doorknob before she yelped with pain. He'd tried to weld the door shut! Sick from the shock, she ran back to the bathroom to run cold water over her hand. It hurt so much she cried. White blisters rose on two fingers and her right thumb.

Ten minutes later, blisters bandaged, armed with a thick towel, she tried the door again. The towel scorched, but the door wouldn't budge. She decided to try the service hall door in the study but with no real hope.

To her surprise, that door hadn't been touched. He must have thought it was a closet, she decided, cautiously stepping into the narrow hall. Everything looked normal. Night lights were on. All was quiet. A breeze swept through the room, the draft from the open window.

Down the hall the door to Worth's apartment stood open; lights were on, but there wasn't a sound. Merry waited, tiptoed closer, then went in. The shabbily furnished apartment was tiny— two small rooms and a bath. The bed hadn't been slept in. Worth's clothes and personal things were gone. Drawers hung open. The bathroom had been stripped of towels. Three hairs curled in the sink. The digital timer on the door lock said 1:05.

That Worth and the stranger might have taken the aircar did not occur to her until she had reached the corridor. Her slowness wasn't due to stupidity but to the knowledge that such an act on Worth's part would end not only the woman's career but, considering whose car it was, possibly her life. Was Worth so terrified of Mikel that she would agree to anything? Merry could understand that; a person might say or do anything to avoid being burned. The thing now was to see if her grandfather was still here.

The only movement in the dim corridor was a rover unit polishing the floor, its rotary pads whirling noiselessly. All seemed to be as it should in the house at this time of night. The idea that Worth and the boy might have gone was comforting, and Merry relaxed enough to remember she didn't need to tiptoe in soft-soled shoes. Tiptoeing made her legs ache.

Ahead of her the rover came to a stop, backed up, and folded its pads beneath itself. A red light atop its canister began to blink, as if the unit feared ramming a human. She could see a loglike object lying on the floor, which was an odd place for a log—and something gold gleaming, like a coin. She stopped and picked up the gold. It was an SSF collar insignia. She quickly turned away, not wanting to see more clearly what she'd mistaken for a log. A wave of nausea swept over her, and she began to run, wanting to be far from *that* if she fainted.

The ornate doors of the master suite stood open to the corridor, as did the doors beyond into the receiving room. The place had been vandalized: flowers thrown, vases smashed, water streaking down walls. A long burn mark furrowed a priceless silk tapestry. A thirtieth-century stone religious carving had been thrown through the aquarium. The white carpet sparkled with shards of wet glass mixed with exotic fish, their brilliant colors fading in death.

Merry took in all this ruin and more without really seeing it, hurrying through the rooms, afraid of what she'd find. The only reassuring thing was that this suite didn't have that sickening smell the hall did.

The bedroom especially had been vandalized—furniture overturned and broken, things ripped off the walls, burns from a laser pistol marring what was too large to move. Beside the bed was her grandfather's watch. Someone had ground a boot heel into its ruby face. When she picked it up, the hands dropped off, fragile golden arrows lost in the carpet.

In the dressing room and closet, which was large enough to house a family, little had been spoiled because it was nearly empty. She was just about to leave when there was a noise from inside the fur vault. Two months before, when she'd explored this suite, that vault had been empty. Tiptoeing closer, she pressed her ear against the wall. At first all she heard was her own heartbeat in her ears, then the faint brush of bare feet on wood. Someone was hiding in there. Thinking it must be one of the servants, she tugged open the heavy door.

At the rear of the narrow cedar-lined safe stood her grandfather, looking as if he expected the worst. He was clad only in a white silk nightshirt that ended at his knees. She'd seen him always dressed in the dignity of his uniform or in formal attire. Now he looked oddly diminished and old, his legs too thin, his shoulders smaller. The cold overhead light revealed sprouting whiskers that blurred the studied effect of his beard, deepening each wrinkle and shadow.

As they stared at one another, his expression changed from numbed stoicism to relief to irritation. "You'll have to excuse my informal appearance," he said. "I hadn't expected guests."

"They're gone, I think." She stepped aside to let him out.

"Put shoes on. There's glass all over the floor."

"Are you unharmed?" He didn't wait for her answer but hurried directly to his clothing.

She considered her bruises, burned hand, and fear. "Yes, sir. Almost."

"Ah. I'm going to kill her, you know."

"Who?"

"Your bodyguard."

"For what she did to me or for what they did to your aide?" she asked, wondering how he knew.

"What was that?"

He sounded only politely interested, preoccupied with other matters. As she told him what had happened, she could hear him getting dressed, then the murmur of his razor as he shaved. Somehow it seemed an odd time to worry about personal appearance, and she wondered if he were listening to her. She sat down on the jumble of bedding and pulled a torn brown satin comforter over her legs. Bits of goose down puffed out and went floating off like thistle seeds.

"And you didn't see the weapon this fellow used?" Ambrose called after she'd fallen silent.

"He doesn't use any. Just his hands."

"Wrong!" He corrected her with quiet surety. "He has to have a weapon. You just didn't see it. My office is running an ID check. We'll know who he is by morning."

"How?" she said. "Your aircar's gone. This house doesn't even have a radio."

"Ah. You're right. Awkward."

He emerged from the dressing room wearing uniform trousers, high black boots, beige tunic, belt. The tunic had a laser scorch across one sleeve. "She didn't leave me much," he explained, seeing Merry's frown, then changed the subject. "Where did he tell you he came from?"

"Teratu." He gave her a sharp, questioning look. "I think that's in the South Pacific," she added helpfully, "and he said he was going to rule the Earth, that Worth said he could."

"Insane. Both of them." He stooped and picked up the torso of a tiny bronze warrior, shield flush to its side. "Six thousand years old and she destroys it." He sighed. "How do you deal with a mind like that?"

"Why were you hiding in the fur vault?" The question was tactless, but she wanted to know.

"It seemed prudent at the time. I was in the bathroom, heard a scream in the corridor, and came out to see your bodyguard run into the lobby, gun in hand. She didn't seem friendly, and there was no way to escape or get my gun without being seen, so I retreated to the vault."

"What if she'd found you there?"

"I'd be dead," he said matter-of-factly. He went over to a window and ran his hand beneath the sill. A concealed panel bin dropped open to reveal two small but wicked-looking handguns. "Want one?" he offered.

"I don't know how to use it."

"Then you're safer without it." He put a gun in either side pocket of his tunic. "Come along now. We'll go see what's going on. I imagine most of the excitement is over or someone would have come by this time. We're extremely lucky the house didn't catch fire."

It just occurred to her. "How do you know it was just Worth? This is a lot of damage for one person."

"Worth? Is that her name?" He smiled wryly. "She may have had help, but she was the only one I saw, there"—he pointed to the shattered mirror wall—"before I hid. She put her defensive training to good use, I can tell you. That table was split with one kick, that chair with the side of her foot." He picked up a slender curved chair leg and laid it on the bed. "What frightened me most was her anger. Her cold rage. She has no cause to hate me. She's lived well in our service." He caught her glance. "Yes, I was afraid," he admitted. "As frightened as you were outside that window. Never be afraid to admit fear, but only to yourself, of course. Stupid bravery gets you killed. Death ends the game. You lose."

The corridor was quiet. The robo-polisher had given up hope of the obstruction's moving and had circled away and gone on with its work. Ambrose gave the charred remains of his aide a cursory inspection and hurried on without comment. Afterward

Merry remembered that he showed regret only for the destruction of artworks and antiques. The dead left him unmoved. Each time he passed a wall intercom, he stopped and tried to use it. None worked. After the second try he carried one of the guns in hand and warned her, "If I have to fire, you get behind me. No questions."

"Yes, sir."

He went directly to the building's control room, where the house computer was located. The steel door marked "Authorized Personnel Only" hung ajar. When he pushed it open, the acrid smell of plastic was choking. Merry had never seen the room before and could only guess at its normal appearance. All the equipment had been melted into misshapen lumps, charred and ruined.

For the first time her grandfather seemed shaken and kept looking from the melted equipment to the ceiling. "Why didn't the fire alarm go off? Why didn't the sprinklers go on? How could this happen?"

"The things he burns don't give off much heat," Merry explained. "At least not the ones I saw. They seem to burn so quickly that no energy is lost." She was going to relate more of her observations, but her grandfather waved his hand for silence and said he wanted to think. "If they've taken my aircar, as you say, I could be trapped here, a sitting duck for some plot. . . ." He pulled the door shut behind him and stood pondering.

Merry leaned against the wall to consider this and decided that would mean she was a sitting duck, too, if anyone cared enough to bother. She was suddenly very tired and cold. She'd never warmed up properly after her drenching, her hair was still damp, and there was a draft in the halls. Minutes passed, and she had just decided to go back to her room for a sweater when General Ambrose barked, "Come!" and set off toward the staff quarters. "I might as well find out where I stand, if it's the start

73

H. M. Hoover

of a revolution or the spite work of one malcontent." He glanced
back over his shoulder at her. "Where did he tell you he came
from?"

"Teratu." Then she remembered. "He said something about
our thinking it was a moon because we were ignorant."

"Ah!" He nodded to himself as if that meant something. "He
has to be lying, of course."

As they passed the room where Mikel Goodman had been
held, she detoured over and opened the door, then wished she
hadn't. At her sharp little "oh!" of horror, General Ambrose
turned, gun ready, then saw what she had found. He stepped
past her into the room and hit the alarm button. Nothing happened. He shouted for help.

74

chapter VIII

HAD THEY ASKED, A COMPUTER IN THE CORE LAB OF THE Shepherd Moon could have told them that the sole surviving member of Project Earthfall was moving at great speed across a continent. The signal from the transmitter buried in Mikel's thigh remained strong even as the distance from the planet lengthened. But no one asked.

The governing committee was busy deciding how they would explain the absence of Terra IV. To ease acceptance by their people, certain drugs would be added to the food supply. When time enough had passed for the drugs to take effect, an announcement would be made that, due to unexpected structural changes in their hull, the people of Terra IV had been relocated, along with their possessions. No one would be unduly inconvenienced by the change, the becalmed listeners would be assured. In each world they would assume the other worlds played host.

Life within The Shepherd Moon went on undisturbed. On schedule the silver, gold, or pastel rains were set to fall on the greens between the habitats. The Bells of Three-On chimed the start of each new day; Three Shift began work as Two Shift began their leisure and One prepared for sleep. In the nurseries the beautiful babies played or slept or listened to the murmur of their mamatrons.

From the aircar's window Mikel could see a white cloud floor below and stars far overhead. The view gave him a terrifying sense of height. He'd never flown before. No-grav games didn't count, and he'd been unconscious in the capsule until the sensors woke him to the pitch of waves. He didn't like flying, not at all. The speed, the hiss of air passing this odd little room, being told he couldn't get out until they "landed," all was stressful and made him feel helpless.

Worth sat at the controls. He didn't like that, either; that gave her control over him. He'd had enough of that. But at the moment he had no choice. She'd made his vulnerability clear. "If anything happens to me, you'll be shot within a week, if not sooner. You don't know how to act, how to survive. You'd terrify people and give yourself away."

She was correct, of course. The entertainment channels his world monitored from Earth had provided him with only one truly useful thing: language and accent. The people and the way they lived bore no relation to those plays. They were not dumpy and dough-faced, did not wear shiny bright clothing, didn't laugh all the time. He'd seen no one who was mentally retarded and spoke only in shouts, as Earthlings did in their plays.

Worth began talking to someone, but there was no face on her screen. What she said made no sense, being mostly letters and numbers in sequence. Another woman's voice began repeating similar things. Worth listened intently and tapped on a keyboard. When he laughed and tried to join the game, she slapped his hand away and told him to "Shut up and sit still!"

Then he understood she had no real respect for him at all. She was like his group leader, who liked you only when you did exactly as ordered. Very well. He would wait and watch and learn to survive. There would come a time when he wouldn't need her anymore. Still, she understood what it was like to be superior and treated always as a tool. She knew what he felt, and she felt the same.

He stretched out in the seat and closed his eyes. It had been a busy time after so much inactivity. If only he'd been able to convert that child. That was Worth's fault. If he hadn't listened to Worth, the child would have never wakened. All the rest had gone so smoothly. Just that one mistake. Unless Worth had made some? She seemed angry about something.

They had been so bored, his guards; it was easy to amuse them, to make them laugh and tell him stories. These people liked to talk about themselves, to star in their own lives. The more they told him, the better they liked and trusted him, and they never knew what they truly liked was their reflection mirrored in his eyes. They never seemed to realize that they didn't know him at all. So long as he was beautiful and listened and did not threaten their fantasy.

When they let him leave his room and showed him where and how they lived, all they wanted was to have their accomplishments acknowledged. Poor simple, trusting people. The guards at home trusted no one. When he sympathized with Worth's story of injustice and told her what he could do if people treated him like that, she had believed him because she wanted to, because she wanted power.

After the men in gray-and-black uniforms left his room, he had asked for Worth, and when she came, he whispered to her of his fear. She shot out the camera's eye. They were just about to leave when a gray officer returned, insolent and cold, calling him a liar, ordering Worth from the room. Worth had struck the man unconscious and removed his suit. "No one questions the right of an SSF officer to go anywhere," she'd said, and made him put it on. The cloth smelled disgusting, of sweat and alien food. Worth called him hypersensitive, but she was used to Earthly stinks. Those creatures called pigs, for example, had smelled so bad that he gagged thinking about them.

A guard had run in, half-dressed. The sound of the camera going off had triggered a silent alarm. A second guard soon followed. Mikel smiled, remembering the look on their faces when they saw him in his uniform. Like Lexus, they didn't want to understand—or join and free themselves from servitude. He'd held out his hands to them—made them both examples. They didn't have enough air to scream, or enough time. Worth said what remained would have great psychological impact. She appeared to be surprised when he actually did it—impressed but not pleased—perhaps because not all the men's mass changed form. Only the plant in the child's room had converted as it should. The people left a lot of residue. That wasn't supposed to happen. He wasn't sure if the problem was Earth's atmosphere or perhaps the different diet. Or even himself; perhaps he wasn't able to focus properly here? Still, the plant had converted instantly. But the equipment merely melted. He would have to practice.

"Firebird, this is Phoenix. Bring your present home. Eight-oh-one to four key. Nine-nine-nine to one. Run silent from now on."

Worth was looking at him, a strange expression on her face, then asked if he was hungry. It would be a long trip, she said.

"Are you afraid of me?" he asked, accepting a dry cracker.

"I'd be a fool if I weren't."

chapter IX

MERRY WOKE ON THE WINDOW SEAT, THE SUN WARM ON HER legs. For a moment she couldn't think why she was in the library, sleeping in her clothes. Turning carefully on the narrow cushion brought to view white puffy clouds drifting high over the tops of red maple trees. Seagulls wheeled, making high, thin cries. A bluejay darted past the window. Remembering, she sat up. Outside, everything looked scrubbed and clean. With sunshine the night seemed like a bad dream.

In the dither that had followed the discovery of the burned bodies, she had been ignored. She had stood in the hall for a while, watching and trying to keep out of the way. For a time everyone had talked and nobody listened. "Didn't you hear anything?" they asked one another accusingly. "How could this happen?" The ground crew came in and hurried to tell how the aircar had suddenly taken off, and how they had found the estate's two airtrucks smoldering in the hangar, ruined. Their discovery made them feel important, part of the drama. This tragedy was the first truly interesting thing to have happened to them in years, Merry decided.

They dismissed the stranger as a minor mystery, a victim somehow of Worth. They all believed Worth had done these terrible things with a high-powered laser. The fact that none had ever seen a gun capable of such an effect didn't sway opinion. "She'd keep it hidden, wouldn't she?" Her treating them like country bumpkins rankled, and they wanted to believe the worst of her.

Her grandfather didn't tell them what Merry had seen, and he interrupted her when she tried to talk. "They won't believe you," he whispered, "and I don't want them to start thinking." Instead he told them he could only suspect the pair of being part of a revolutionary group bent on his assassination. At that all had quieted; if there was a revolution, their own lives and comfort might be jeopardized.

When a lift truck came down the hall with wooden boxes on its hoist, Merry left. She didn't want to see how they would clear those bodies off the floor. The idea of spending the night alone in her rooms was frightening, and there was still that body in the corridor outside the master suite. She wandered back to the library, for want of a safer place. The blanket still lay in the chair; the tea cart remained, forgotten by Williams. She poured herself some brandy, mixed in cold tea, and swallowed the stuff like medicine to get warm, then curled up with the blanket, a burning stomachache, and a foul taste in her mouth.

Now, staring out at the distant whitecaps sparkling in the sun, she felt depressed. She couldn't pretend this early in the morning. She didn't matter to anyone, except as a convenience or a bother. And those who mattered to her didn't care that they did. Not really. If she hadn't been able to save herself last night, no one would have known until it was too late, or even cared much, except that they were responsible for her and would be reprimanded for her loss.

Outside, the bluejays made a ruckus, diving at a herring gull standing on the lawn. The gull stood secure and self-satisfied. No other gull looked at it. None came to its defense or screamed at its attackers. It ignored the feisty jays until they grew too bold, then calmly took wing and flew off toward the barns. Alone.

She admired gulls without liking them—they were elegant fliers but a greedy, squabbling lot in crowds. Yet in her present mood she identified with this one. "I matter to myself," she said aloud, and got up and folded the blanket. Having made this decision, she paused. Mattering only to one's self was cold comfort. It also seemed to be what everybody here did best. At that thought her mind regained its balance, and she grinned.

Sporadic hammering and the whine of a sander greeted her as she came up the ramp. Repairmen were working. The air smelled of soap and disinfectant. The ruined doors had been removed. A strip of flooring was gone from the place where the charred body had lain the night before. A sawhorse stood guard across the gap in the marble. Workmen glanced up as she passed, and looked surprised to see her. She didn't wave or say good morning as she would have yesterday. There was no point in pretending they were friends. They weren't.

Her rooms still smelled of burned plastic, but the little study already had been stripped bare, rug and all; a new intercom unit lay on a new bedside table. A draft from the bathroom window had scattered and dried the leaves she'd brought in on her feet the night before. Her reflection in the mirrors looked unfamiliar, as if her face didn't quite belong to her but perhaps to one of the paintings in the gallery.

She had just finished brushing her teeth when she heard voices in the corridor. Thinking it was the workmen, she hurried out to close the bedroom door.

"She didn't say where she'd been?" General Ambrose called.

"No, sir, but she didn't look happy."

"Few of us do this morning. Meredith?" Catching sight of her, he paused and turned to call, "Bring us breakfast, Williams. Coffee, eggs, and toast with lots of honey."

"To this suite, sir?"

"As soon as you can."

"Yes, sir." Williams, who always insisted Merry eat in the dining room, hurried off without a murmur.

"Now," the general said, addressing her. "Where were you last night?"

"I slept in the library."

"Ah." It was a sigh of understanding. "I suppose one could." The chair cushion sighed as he sank down, looking tired. He was still wearing the same clothing, creased now and stained, and his boots needed polishing. "Would you mind closing the door?"

She did so, wondering what was coming.

"I must apologize for my brusqueness last night." He paused to gently massage the puff under his right eye. "You see, I didn't want you to say things that would further alarm the staff or cause them to ask awkward questions. I doubt that any of them would recognize the name Terra II, but one never knows."

"Please," Merry said. "I don't understand."

"No." He rubbed his eye again. "I don't either. But I've talked with the house physician and watched two autopsies. That was no weapon we have; they burned as if the body's liquid were gasified and ignited instantly . . . there may be a chance he wasn't lying, that he came from Terra II. All the information on him was destroyed with the computer. We don't even have a picture. It's highly unlikely, of course, that anyone still lives on The Shepherd Moon."

She didn't know what he was talking about, so she remained silent. Through the closed door came the rasp of fabric being pulled from a wall. General Ambrose sat brooding, his forefingers making a church steeple above the roof of his clasped hands.

"You must draw me a picture of the thing he arrived in, the pillows, as you call them. We must learn if an envelope could protect a body in a vacuum. If it can, it's my guess it was one of several packed into your big maple key. Seeds in a seedpod, as it were. If so, did others fall? Draw me the maple key as well. . . . I wonder why she thinks he can be all-powerful, if there's a reason, or if she is merely ignorant. What else can he do besides that revolting magic trick?"

He glanced at Merry, saw he had totally confused her, and smiled apologetically. "Perhaps I'd better explain. Look out there, at the ocean. There was a bay there once, some miles out, and the port of a great city. This house stands atop its suburbs. The islands to the south mark its center; their base is the rubble of Boston. Have you heard that name?"

She shook her head.

"Few have," he conceded. "It's forgotten—like New York or Rome or the Kingdom of Kush. But once thousands of people lived on this land. There were great universities. From them came the initial plans for a series of satellite colonies to orbit Earth. Almost a hundred were completed by the thirty-first century—seventeen hundred years ago. The oldest and greatest of them was called Terra II. The next was Terra III, and so on."

Merry had been searching for one of her sketch pads, half-distracted, but at that name she looked up sharply. "Terra II? It's a moon? A—" She remembered the picture of Earth with two moons—realized then it was an historic photo of that first colony.

He nodded. "It's not a Pacific island as you guessed, but the largest of the remaining space colonies. People called it The Shepherd Moon, a poetic name indicating its mastery and guardianship over the others." He smiled to himself. "The shepherds in this case used a military staff to guide their flock. That's where Earth erred. Power once given—"

"People *live* inside the moons? It's *possible* he came from there?" Merry asked, trying to accept the idea, intrigued by it. "They're not true moons?"

"What you saw crash offshore was a shell fragment of the colony Terra IV. The telescope on Mount Elbrus saw it struck by an asteroid."

"With people inside?"

Ambrose shrugged. "We don't know. When the *moons* are near Earth, as now, telescopes can see lights on their hulls. But those could be solar powered and burn forever, untended. The fragments the salvage ship recovered were metallic ash." He shifted in the chair and settled himself more comfortably. "What you must understand from all this ancient history is that perhaps a thousand years ago those colonies rebelled against Earth and declared their independence. At that time, Earth had vast solar collectors in space—to supply electrical power. Colonial forces either destroyed these or turned them into weapons against us. The lights went out on Earth. In the war that followed, Earth destroyed some of the colonies and blasted others into new orbits. They retaliated by burning a large portion of Earth. We don't know how at this point—perhaps we never did. The polar ice caps began to melt; the climate changed; the oceans rose. At that time, most of the world's people lived along the coasts. People fled inland as the cities drowned. In addition to fire and flood, there was starvation, chaos, disease. Earth's human population was reduced to what it had been in the fourteenth century. The period was called the Second Dark Age. And it was, almost literally. There was social and economic collapse. Too few people survived to do the work that had to be done, and the succeeding generations forgot most of what their ancestors knew."

"How terrible!"

"At the time, yes. In the long term I suspect they did us a

favor," he said. "In one step they reduced our population to manageable numbers. If that disaster hadn't happened, perhaps a different and ultimately more terrible one would have." He chuckled humorlessly. "At any rate, the Dark Age made possible the Ambrose family as we are today."

Merry ignored that, preoccupied by the idea of inhabited moons. "The people in the colonies," she said. "What happened to them after the war? Did anyone go see?"

"Possibly. But those shuttle ports not destroyed were abandoned for lack of maintenance—or so I would imagine. Earth's survivors had other things to worry about. By the fortieth century most of the colonies had disappeared. Scholars believe some collided with orbiting debris. It doesn't matter now."

"Doesn't . . ." She hesitated, unsure how to ask her question. "Can't we try to contact them? If there's anybody out there—"

"It's been tried. Not lately, I admit, but only for lack of response. It's possible, of course, that they want nothing more to do with us—that life still exists and is more advanced than ours. If those remaining colonies lost nothing in the wars and kept on learning . . . We regressed. We're still relearning and re-inventing things we knew long before we built the moons. They might know a thousand things we've yet to learn."

"Do you think so?"

"Officially? No. We've long assumed the moons were empty hulks." He met her questioning frown and confided, "When I was young, I used to dream of going up there someday . . . entering The Shepherd Moon, finding the remains of a civilization in vast dark echoing spaces. Skeletons lying on broad stairs. Shutters open on the Milky Way, jewelry lying in the dust."

"How would we get there?" she asked, taken with the idea.

"Ah, that's the problem. That's part of the knowledge we've lost—and which, incidentally, it is official policy to have remain lost. We have no aircraft powerful enough to free us from Earth's gravity, or to protect us from its fatal pull when we return." He stared at her without seeing, lost in some idea, and then abruptly shook his head and became all business again. "Which is just as well. There are things people shouldn't know. Things that would simply confuse and frighten them." His eyes bored into hers for a moment. "What I've told you will go no further than this room? Is that understood?"

"Yes, sir."

"Good." His face relaxed again. "It hasn't been high-priority information. This is the first moon fragment to hit Earth in three hundred years."

Williams came then with their breakfast. As the table was being set, the general said he was going to drive to the nearest town and commandeer an aircar to take him home. "You're welcome to come with me," he assured her. "I'd appreciate the company. But before you say yes, you'd better know the only transport Worth left us is the old beach car. It's hardly luxury stuff, and the trip may take several days."

"Thank you! I'd like to go."

chapter X

AT THE FOOT OF THE HILL WHERE THE GRAVEL DRIVEWAY
met the freight road, Merry turned and looked back. From this
distance, with sheep grazing on the lawn, the old house seemed
to dream in the last sunshine of high autumn, secure and peaceful, beyond time. For a moment she felt she didn't want to go,
ever, that like her great-grandmother she should stay here where
the days were as quiet as those countless empty rooms and people
were remembered by portraits in the halls. The beach car bumped
up onto the worn tarmac and rolled through a gate she'd never
noticed. A wall shut off her view.

The road cut like a firebreak through the forest, which covered
most of the estate. The scents of humus and autumn leaves
replaced the smell of the sea. Leaves on the road whirled in the
car's wake; others drifted down, sailing lazily in the sunshine.

Twenty miles west of the house another road joined this one.
It led northeast but was half-choked by encroaching trees. "That
leads to the Otabai estate," the general said in answer to her
question. "There's not much left there now. Once it was the

showplace of the coast. When I was small, I could see its lights on a clear night—like a beacon in the distance." He fell silent for a moment, remembering. Merry waited. "The house burned years ago. I was at the party there the night it happened. . . . Avril Otabai set it on fire. She was my first wife, you know."

"On purpose?"

"The fire or the wife?"

"The fire," she said, grinning.

"It was deliberately set. She said she was tired of living with ghosts."

"Why not move? Why burn it?"

He smiled slowly, not at her but at an image somewhere down the road in the past. "It seemed a good idea at the time."

"Oh," she said. Grandfather's first wife was a taboo subject at home. "I never met her."

"No." He swerved as three pheasants flushed from cover and flew across the road. "You never did."

"Where is she now? Do you know?"

Between sunglasses, beard, and a gardener's cap with a visor to shield his eyes, she couldn't see enough of his face to gauge his reaction, but by the time he answered, she had grown uneasy, afraid that she had trespassed on his sense of privacy. "She's at Easthaven," he said finally. "In the family crypt. They found her body on the beach one morning. She'd been swimming. She and the baby. Apparently, both drowned."

"I'm sorry," she said automatically, shocked by that unexpected bit of family history. She'd always thought his first wife left him, as his second had. That was what she'd overheard her father say once.

"Yes. It was very sad." He'd used the words so often that all the feeling had been worn out. "That was a long time ago."

Apparently, both drowned? Wasn't he sure? Curious as she was, she decided not to pry. She disliked people who asked her questions she didn't want to answer. If he wanted to tell her more, he would; and if he didn't, she would do some research on her own.

With both lost in their own thoughts, an hour passed before he broke the silence by asking if she drove. "Yes," she said. "Worth taught me this summer." He stopped and exchanged seats with her and, with what she considered touching trust in her limited driving experience, he almost instantly fell asleep.

She was glad to drive, not only for the fun of it. The fat wheels and suspension that made this aged vehicle perfect on the beach made it less than perfect on this road. At its top speed of thirty-five miles per hour the car tended to sway up and down in a way that did strange things to her stomach. Driving kept her mind from thoughts of motion sickness.

The road wound through the hills, now climbing, now descending. There was no traffic, no people, nothing but trees. A fox sat beneath a sumac and watched her pass. On a grassy bank a fat woodchuck stood sentry. Here and there trees had fallen in the storm and had to be gotten around. The roughest bumps over broken limbs and rocks barely roused the general, and he immediately went back to sleep, once sure that she was managing. She decided he'd been up more than one night to get so tired.

By October's early sunset she was cold and stiff from sitting. She'd worn her warmest jacket, but it had never been intended for driving in an open car on an autumn day. She drove on because she didn't know what else to do. Mist rose and drifted above the road. Finally shivering made necessary a stop and a discreet trip into the bushes.

The general was standing by the car when she returned. "Listen to the silence," he called as she made her way down the sumac-grown bank. "You can hear a leaf break free and float away. That's what woke me, the silence—and a leaf skating on the road." As they stood there, Merry realized how accustomed she'd become to the surf as background noise. Without it something was missing—like the stillness in a room when a clock stops ticking.

"We'd better camp soon," he said. "There's no light on this vehicle." He looked up and down the road. "If I recall my landmarks, there's a lake not far ahead—if it hasn't silted to swamp."

"How long ago did you drive through here?"

"Twenty or thirty years," he said easily as he slid into the driver's seat.

She shivered and hugged her jacket close as she got in. For some reason his answer made her lonely. To think of her grandfather driving here before she was born, before her father was as old as she was now, gave her a sense of perspective she didn't particularly like. Life went on whether one was there or not.

"Come," he said, studying her face. "You need some hot food."

The lake he remembered was now a marshy pond, mirrored gold by twilight and rimmed by reeds and cattails. They parked on a strip of broken paving, put there for the truckers' use, he told her. "This was originally called the Dirt Road. It was used to haul topsoil to the estates along the coast, and afterward for freight and produce before airtrucks made life easy. Now it's rarely used. I have it kept clear out of sentiment."

From beneath the canvas over the freight bed he removed hampers and bedrolls and quickly set up a rude camp. "I'd build a fire for the warmth, but on the long chance that someone wants to kill me, a fire would be a beacon to an aircar," he explained apologetically.

They dined on beef stew from a thermos, and chunks of crusty butter bread, their dishes large tin cups, their utensils round-bowled spoons. Her bath was limited to washing her face and hands in the pond. The water smelled of plants and mud. It was so dark by then that she couldn't tell what animal made the splashing noises on the far bank. By the time she had removed her muddy boots and slid into her sleeping bag, her teeth were chattering. Twenty minutes passed before the down warmed her and she began to yawn.

She'd never slept outside before, never seen so many stars. One lone cricket sang. Were there snakes this time of year? Someone said once that snakes liked to curl up on a camper's neck to keep warm at night. The general had placed the sleeping bags on opposite sides of the car, saying, "We're both accustomed to privacy." At the time she'd been glad. Now she wasn't so sure.

She peered beneath the car and saw him as a silent shape darker than the night. The car was clicking to itself as if it too were settling down to rest after its longest run in years. The wheel motor beside her was warm to the touch.

Either a muskrat or a fish splashed in the pond. Something was walking in the leaves with stealthy little pawsteps. Another creature bounced along—were squirrels up after dark? Birds twittered in the pines off to the right. From high in the northern sky came the sudden gabble of wild geese. Merry glanced up and saw a falling star, then another and another, tiny arcs of yellow, great slashes of blues and greens and violets that seemed to explode and flare like some incredibly distant fireworks. With each bright flash the wild geese commented excitedly until their unseen flock passed beyond hearing. Still the stars fell.

"Are you awake and watching?"

Her grandfather's voice made her jump; she'd forgotten everything for minutes.

"Yes."

"It's quite awesome, isn't it?"

"Is that the Orionid shower?" That was the only autumnal meteor group she could remember.

"Ah, I believe this one's unscheduled, the remains of Terra IV, or its inhabitants. Or both. We'd have seen them nights before and possibly more spectacularly if there'd been no clouds."

"Do you really think some of them are people?" That idea bothered her.

"It would be a good way to go," he said. "One final blaze of glory."

What would it feel like to be that high and falling? she wondered. But of course you'd never know; you'd be dead. Did you get to heaven faster if you died in space? It would be interesting to discuss the subject with him, but he might think it was silly or infantile. She doubted that he believed in heaven—most people didn't—but she rather liked the idea. It was a very old myth, and she'd often wondered where it came from. Where among the stars was heaven? Or was it beyond? Hell was easy to understand; people had created that so often here on Earth. And perhaps in the heavens too if Mikel came from there. To end in fire . . . she shuddered at the thought.

"Are you still cold?" the general asked, concerned. "Would you like a blanket?"

"No, I scared myself, that's all."

"Ah . . . good night."

Beneath the pale haze of the Milky Way the meteoroids winked and flared until the old moon rose and dimmed the more distant stars. After midnight three slivers of moons rose, small gray-blue Cheshire cat's smiles that might pass unnoticed unless watched for. From his bed beside the car August Ambrose watched and knew that he was seeing them for the last time in his life.

Whatever they might be, by the time their orbit brought them back to Earth again, he would be gone. Or one hundred and sixty years old. The last time they appeared, his parents had been young and he was merely part of their future. The next time . . . he looked over at the sleeping girl . . . she would be old then if life was kind to her. He got up quietly and walked around the car to cover her with an extra blanket, thinking that she was perhaps the last hope he had for the future. Or his last illusion.

Far to the southwest and hours later Mikel saw the moons. He stood alone and disappointed in the street of a desert village. The land around him had been sea bottom aeons before and would be so again, aeons hence. He didn't know that or care. He hated the place. It frightened him. It was huge and empty and silent, hot by day and cold by night. From horizon to horizon there was nothing but sky, and all around nothing but sand and rocks and twisted dry vegetation. And insects, disgusting little creatures with lots of hairy legs. Until Worth had brought him here, he'd never seen an insect, never known there were such things. And she said the bite of some could cause pain and death. Why did these stupid people allow insects to live? How dare she bring him here? He hated her, too!

They were all afraid of him. And their fear made them dangerous. He'd been good. He'd shown them what he could do— or most of it. It was all Worth's fault. She had promised.

After all his years of training she and these pathetic people were going to teach him how to act? They made him wear their ugly garments that chafed his skin. Their drinking water had a nasty taste. Their food was revolting. They hid here like criminals, all their equipment stolen. They smelled of sweat and talked of revolution and their own superiority—yet not one was smart enough to trust him or to be trusted. And they were going to teach him?

Worth and the others said there were cities, that the pictures on the screens each night came from there, that in time, when he had learned how to act, they would take him there. Then his face would appear on the screen and all the world would come to love him for his beauty. Worth and her people would teach him what to say. He would be their symbol of a better world to come, and they were right, of course. But it would be his world, not theirs.

They talked of his power to charm, to make people believe what they wanted them to. But if he did as they wanted, he would be controlled again. They kept saying they could "use" him. That wasn't what Worth had promised. She'd said he could rule the world, and he knew he could. If he had access to a studio and all that equipment, he wouldn't need her words. He could call them all to him, mix his own acoustics, make them do as *he* wanted. He would control as he was trained to do. And if any of the other cadets had survived, they would come to him and serve him as Master until the Shepherds came with all their people. That wasn't part of his commands, but why else would they order him to survive? They would be so pleased to find everyone here docile. But when would they come? Do not doubt. Do not question.

He was so hungry.

Space didn't look familiar from the planet's surface. It was more blue than black, even at night. All the stars were in the wrong places. He stared up at The Shepherd Moon and thought of his instructors. They were good, but he was better; he was sure of that. Good enough to keep them ignorant of how good he was.

He was free to be himself, to do as he wished. A vague, uneasy thought flickered in his mind; perhaps his instructors had guessed— that's why he was one of those chosen for this mission? Any person would have done, with death so probable. Why send their best Controller? Because he was the best? Because they knew he would survive? Was this an experiment? A test? Would they come here if they could? It was an ugly place.

A coyote howled in the darkness beyond the village, a wild

cry that sent shivers through him. He didn't know what it was; perhaps a human made that sound? Someone condemned to live here for life? But the people here were sleeping, ignorant of shifts. They wouldn't be out howling.

There was no point in wasting time. He went in to wake up Worth. It was time they heard the singing.

chapter XI

FROM EARLY MORNING THEY'D BEEN DRIVING THROUGH A pine forest. The trees were all identical, spaced to march in rows. A freight rail curved down a hill to run beside the road. Twice a flatcar passed, on automatic glide, carrying logs to a mill somewhere ahead, trailing a smell of freshly cut pine.

The road now was so rough that Merry found it hard to keep her seat. Bumps tossed her up toward the roll cage; tightening the seat belts bruised her shoulders. She was silently vowing to make all future trips by air when she noticed people working in a line across a bald hill. They were the first humans she'd seen in almost twenty-four hours, and she found the sight cheering. "What are they doing, stooping and hunching like that?"

"Mulching seedlings planted among old stumps," her grandfather answered.

"Isn't there an easier way?"

"There is, but none that keeps so many people busy." He glanced over at her. "Work gives people a sense of purpose—identity. They become their jobs. . . ." His voice trailed away, and the car slowed. Merry followed his gaze.

A group of joggers was coming down the road. Behind them, like a herd car, crept a small yellow vehicle. After a moment's hesitation he turned the power back on high and drove toward them. The runners didn't move over, and he swerved onto the rough, then stopped and waited for the oncoming car.

It was hard to tell if the runners were male or female. They were a large-hipped, sturdy-looking lot, all young, dressed in pastel sweat suits and cloth shoes that made their feet look big. Their hair was short and shaggy. None was overly clean, and all were sweating.

From the first sign of people Merry had been worrying about her personal appearance. She was grubby; her hair was dusty from the drive, her fingernails gray from washing in the pond. But after catching a downwind from the joggers, she felt comparatively fresh.

As one by one they turned to stare in her direction, she thought of the cattle at Easthaven. Here was the same placid expression, the same mild and impersonal curiosity at the sight of something new. As the cows did when a stranger entered their pasture, this herd came over for a closer look.

"What's wrong with them?" she asked, alarmed, as they drew near the car.

"Nothing," the general assured her. "They're factory workers training for competition. They're perfectly normal." He sounded defensive, and she wondered why.

"Why do they look so simple?"

"Probably the beach car. I'm sure they've never seen one. Or a beach." He eased the car away from an especially curious runner. "You've never been in a flyover area before?"

"What's that?"

"What the term implies, an area we normally never visit so long as it remains stable." She shook her head. "Ah . . . you'll find it educational. Let me do the talking," he cautioned as the yellow car pulled up beside theirs.

"Yo!" The voice identified the plump blond driver as a woman. She wore a brown uniform that labeled her *Security*, and like most people so labeled suggested anything but. "You from one of the estates, old man?"

"Yo," the general responded, and Merry looked at him. Her grandfather saying "Yo" and being addressed as "old man"?

"I thought so if they let you use this road. I'd never work so near the ocean. They say the water's higher every year, drowning more and more."

"So they say," he agreed. "How far do your people run along this road?"

"Not to the restricted zone. Only to the white stones. That your trainee?" The woman pointed to Merry, and without waiting for an answer, decided, "I'd ask for another. This one looks too smart. You get so you can tell who won't work out just by looking at 'em. Someone's been giving this one real meat. What's your classification?"

"Ah . . . you might call me a manager."

"I thought so," the woman said. "What are you doing so far west?"

"Checking for storm damage." He put the car in gear. "We must go. How far is it to Greentown?"

"Five miles to the factory. Two after that. How come they made you drive that ugly thing?"

"It keeps me humble," the general called, and with a brisk wave, moved off.

"They didn't recognize you," Merry said when the joggers had been left behind. He merely smiled and pointed. Beyond the curve ahead, rooftops and factory stacks were coming into view. "Excuse me, sir, but why did those people look like that? Are they retarded?"

"No . . . not literally. They are a bit more—ah—relaxed than their urban counterparts. There's much less stress living out here."

"Easthaven's staff lives in the country, and they don't look like that."

"No," he said vaguely, "they don't. Perhaps it's something in their diet. Meredith, not to change the subject, but we'll soon be reaching civilization again—such as it is—and our private time together will be ending. I want you to know I've enjoyed your company immensely. I was wondering, if it's convenient for both of us, perhaps we could spend a week together at Easthaven in the spring? There are so many things there that I'd like to tell you about, share with you. Someday the house will be yours. You should appreciate its history. . . ."

He did want to change the subject, she knew, but what he said was true, and she felt a very real sense of loss and sorrow that the trip was over. With other people around they couldn't really talk. And she would miss him.

"When in spring?" she asked. She forgot her other questions until there was no time left to ask them.

"Are you arrested?"

Merry heard the whisper twice before suspecting it was being asked of her. She was sitting in the car outside the guard station, waiting for the general. Fifteen minutes had passed since he'd gone inside, and she was getting edgy.

The few people who walked by avoided looking at her. The streets were nearly empty—not that they were real streets, but stretches of bare, rutted ground between the buildings. Trees had sprung up where they could—sycamore, ailanthus, and sugar pine. Goldenrod and asters flourished in untrafficked spots, the only softening touch of color. The residential blocks with their peaked solar roofs looked like enormous poultry sheds. Some of them once were. The whole town smelled of foodstuffs being processed, heavy with spicy flavor and cooking oil. From the distance came a constant low roar of escaping steam mingled with factory noises.

"Are you arrested?" The harsh whisper came again, louder now and closer. She twisted in the seat to look around. Next to the guard station was an abandoned building, its roof caved in, its doors and windows gone. She shielded her eyes against the noon sun, but couldn't see anyone in the dim interior of the ruin.

"You deaf?"

The question came from so close by that she jumped and struck her knee on the dashboard, then jumped again as she saw crouching on the ground beside the car a skinny, dark-haired child of ten or so, with eyes that peered too brightly from a pinched little face. The child wore ragged blue fatigues sizes too large and filthy canvas shoes held on by string wrappings.

"You want to escape?" the ragamuffin asked, exaggerating the words in case Merry had to lip-read. Merry shook her head and smiled, although she wasn't sure the child was playing. "I can help you hide. I'm good at it. I've hid out for a month now. I'm going to find a way home as soon as I find out where I am." At Merry's frown the child added, "It's cold at night and sleeping's hard, but I can take care of myself. You, too, if you want."

"Why are you hiding?" Merry whispered.

The child looked relieved to hear her speak. "I escaped. I'm one of the new conscripts. When I failed my ten-year tests, they sent me here."

"Who did?"

"Soldiers. They pick up conscripts at four in the morning— so nobody sees them."

"What's a conscript?"

The child frowned at her ignorance, then apparently decided

to give her the benefit of the doubt. "Conscripted. You know? Taken away for work duty when there's no jobs in the city? There were three thousand of us on the train—most got taken off before this place. When I got here, they assigned me to the yeast factory, but it's hot and wet and stinky in there."

Pausing as if afraid it had said too much, the child eyed Merry, who stared back in confused concern. This runaway looked as if it hadn't eaten or slept properly in weeks, or had a bath in all that time. What was it Worth had said about her childhood—something about being told she was an orphan? How old had she been then? Her grandfather had to know about such things. "They took three thousand ten-year-olds from the city?"

The child nodded.

"How often does this happen?"

"Every couple of years—" More fear entered the pale face. "How come you don't know that? Where did you come from? If you aren't a prisoner, why don't you get out of the car?" Like an animal sensing danger, it suddenly shrank back against the wheel, then winced and jerked away to crouch on all fours. The wheel was hot.

"Meredith?" the general called as the door to the station slid open. "Would you please come in? The staff artist needs information only you can give him—I never saw the boy—" He paused. "Were you talking to someone?"

From the corner of her eye, she saw the shaggy head frantically shaking no. "Just a sparrow, sir. It's dust-bathing by the car," she said.

"Ah. Come. The car will be quite safe. No one will bother it." He smiled as she got out. "I'm afraid our arrival has upset this station's routine. They have no suitable transportation available. I ordered an airtruck from Hilton so that we can take the beach car. I'd hate to abandon it here. I built it, you know—as a boy." As she came close enough so he could speak without

being overheard, he said, "They didn't believe me when I introduced myself. It was rather awkward. They shoved me to the
Identacom and then learned whom they were bullying." He
chuckled. "The C.O. fears he's jeopardized his career."

"Has he?" Merry asked, not caring, worrying about that child.
Why would it think she'd be a prisoner? Was the child a prisoner—or merely lonely, trying to find a friend? Did ten-year-
olds work?

"Very possibly. His approach at best is overzealous."

Two public vu-phones in the station lobby were situated so
that no call could be kept private. On the wall behind the re-
ception counter, monitoring screens pictured everything from
playgrounds to hallways to warehouse storage areas. Through
one open doorway she could see more screens, through another
a row of metal bars, like the corner of a cage. Perhaps a dozen
guards were about, watching her and the general while pretending to be busy. There was an air of tension in the room.

Ignoring them, the general ushered her into a private office
where an SSF artist waited, on-screen, seated at a drawing board.
As she came within the phone's camera range, the man glanced
up. Twenty minutes later he had, with her help, produced a quite
recognizable likeness of Mikel's face.

"I don't want him hurt," General Ambrose ordered the officer
who replaced the artist on-screen. "I want to interview him personally. And soon. He's to be taken by stun-gun and under no
circumstances allowed to touch anyone. Once he's unconscious,
put him in a straitjacket. Is that clear?"

"Is he contagious, sir? Or insane?"

"No . . . he's expert in a rare form of—uh—martial arts."

"I understand, sir. And the bodyguard?"

"I'll question her too."

He touched the off button, turned in the swivel chair, and

gave her a smile. "We have at least two hours to wait. Would you like to tour the town? It's fairly typical."

"What's a conscript?"

The smile dimmed. "Where did you hear that term? While you waited outside?" She hesitated before nodding. "That's a word we don't use," he said. "Some commoners resent apprenticeship vocational training. They call it by other names. But they must be employed, like all of us. The sooner they learn a skill, the more content they'll be."

"Ten years old?" she said. "Three thousand *ten*-year-olds were taken from the city for job training?"

"At least," he agreed. "From each city. That's about the yearly figure. The population must be kept balanced, Meredith. Life is easier in the cities and more exciting—people crowd there to live. We have to redistribute them somehow or face large masses of unemployed in one area while jobs go begging in another. You'll learn all this in your management courses in the next few years. The details are tiresome, but it's necessary knowledge."

"Why didn't I know about them?"

He smiled slightly. "Because it doesn't concern you. Not as a child. And while it's not publicized, the custom dates back to antiquity. If the State needs workers at Point A and has a surplus at Point B, they move B to A. Mere common sense. And crowded cities lead to crime, terrorism, fires—"

"Nobody *I* know has been conscripted . . ."

That seemed to amuse him, too. "Ah . . . no. That's true. But the people *you* know—or their parents—provide the employment, the food, the housing."

She sensed there was something missing in his logic, but she wasn't sure what.

"What if they don't want to go? The conscripts?"

"Yes, well—some people adapt less readily to the concept of

change, but by the age of ten learning ability can usually be gauged; they haven't reached the age of hooliganism—males are particularly bad for that. . . ."

She listened to him and tried to match this clinical dispassion to the child she'd seen outside, to the runners on the road, to the way this town looked and smelled—and the way she lived.

"It may seem strange to you, Meredith"—his tone broke through her mental fog—"but it is a system we have used for generations. To mitigate it would suggest weakness on the part of the ruling class. That would invite rebellion and chaos. Which comes soon enough in the natural scheme of things. And when the revolution is over, the new ruling class evolves and does much the same as the old. We live in an exhausted world. Not everyone can live well. . . ."

He stared off into space for a moment, suddenly looking old. A buzzer rasped somewhere in the building. Footsteps hurried past the door. "I was lucky in many ways to grow up at Easthaven. In the quiet, where there were other animals besides man to observe and think about. I learned every flock of birds has a strict pecking order. Every dairy herd has its Number One Cow, its Number Two, and so on, and all know their place. Ants and bees are marvels of rigid social order. Social systems are a necessary, natural thing. And so is their collapse." His gaze came back to her. "I have always been glad I was born at the top of ours. So should you be. Your great-grandmother tried to change the world and, failing, returned to Easthaven determined to ignore it. And that, too, was no answer. Enjoy life while you can."

He was telling her not to question, to accept his word, and she was imagining soldiers knocking on her bedroom door at four in the morning, putting her on a train, and sending her to a place like this. A small hard kernel of fear sprouted in the dark of her mind.

"If we didn't conscript children, would we need so many guards?"

"More, I would imagine."

A bell tone chimed, indicating an incoming call. He turned to answer it, and Merry stood up, intending to go out to the car, find the child, and give it the rest of their food. "Please stay." The general pointed to her chair. "I may need your help." She hesitated, then sat down again. Once she gave the child the food, what then? It wouldn't change anything.

"Call on nine, General," a male voice said from the intercom. "Your administrative aide. She says it's urgent."

"Thank you." He pushed a button, and Captain Trask's familiar fox-face appeared on-screen. Merry hadn't seen her for months.

Only a barely perceptible pause and a slight widening of the eyes hinted that his aide found anything odd about the general's costume. "The aircraft in question has been located, General," she announced briskly, "in the West Texas desert. The security officer was found dead. The boy is being flown here to Wheeling. I'll save the details for your arrival."

"Good. He's being taken to Hill Center?"

"No!" Merry interrupted. "You don't want him in the city! What if he gets loose?"

"We've never had an escape from that detention center, sir," the captain said, frowning. She couldn't see who was in the room with her superior. "Is there something we should know about this person?"

"How did Worth die?" asked Merry. "I'll bet—"

"Ah!" The general nodded, understanding, as he interrupted. "Yes, well. How did the bodyguard die, Captain?"

The SSF officer hesitated. "We have no autopsy report as yet, but the patrol who found them claim—let me quote—spontaneous combustion." Her tone indicated what she thought of that. "According to the survivor, she burned in the pilot's seat—but the seat didn't catch fire. It was only charred. She managed to activate the emergency beacon before—"

"He killed her!"

"Sh!" The general hushed Merry. "Captain. Have him flown to Easthaven. In secure restraints, under sedation. I'll meet him there. Now, I'll need some items . . ."

"Aren't you afraid he'll burn Easthaven?" Merry asked when the call ended.

"I'm more afraid what he might say would be heard by too many people."

chapter XII

A STATE TRUCK ARRIVED JUST AT SHIFT CHANGE AND CRE-
ated a dust storm by landing on the worn surface of a playing
field near the guard station. The streets, deserted before, were
now thronged with people. Quietly but persistently they crowded
around the airtruck, as if its coming were a big event. It was all
the guards could do to clear space for the freight ramp to lower
and the beach car to drive on board. There was room for six
beach cars in that hold.

While General Ambrose made sure the car was secured and
said polite good-byes to local officials, Merry went forward into
the passenger compartment. Settling into the plush comfort of
a seat, she looked out the windows. There were children in the
crowd below but not the child she sought. Maybe?

An hour before, with the excuse of being hungry, she had
gone out to the car, gathered up leftover food, and taken it over
to the doorway of the ruined building. There was a path of sorts
through the debris. The place smelled dank, a haunt for spiders
and their ilk. When no one was looking, she had stepped inside

and, placing a cloth napkin over a filthy board, had put down cheese, crackers, and apples. In a loud whisper she'd said, "Hide under the tarp of our car. I'll help you get home." A board creaked somewhere in the dimness. "Are you in here?" There was no answer. The child who was so good at hiding had stayed hidden. She had checked the tarp before they left the station. There were no new bulges. But then why should the child trust her?

On lift-off she watched the crowd recede until their pastel clothes looked like a patch of faded flowers, out of place in autumn. The airtruck banked; the factory section and freight rails came into view and tilted into forested hills. Why didn't the conscripts follow the rails back to the city? But what would they eat along the way? It would be a long, long walk.

The airtruck made their drive seem faintly ridiculous. Twenty minutes after takeoff they landed at Easthaven, with an hour of daylight left. "Won't the staff be pleased," the general joked as he and Merry followed the beach car down the ramp. "Just when they thought the house was theirs again, we come back and bring a dozen more, including a house guest who may be a problem."

Two, she thought, and grinned. The dogs who had come running to greet the strange airtruck were now dancing alongside the beach car as it rolled slowly backward. They were alternately sniffing and woofing and wagging their tails, and both had the peculiarly intent air of animals trying to identify an odor.

"Look at them," the general said. "They smell Greentown on the car. Trust a dog to like stinks. We probably smell of the cooking oil that permeates the air. We'd better bathe immediately or they'll follow and sniff at us. Everything on the car has to be washed and disinfected. Williams!"

At the bottom of the ramp the crewman driving the car braked, afraid she was going to run over a dog. At the hesitation first one dog and then the other jumped up onto the back, barking with renewed excitement. Something beneath the tarp began to kick and thrash about. Bo promptly tried to dig it out.

"You cut that out!" an angry child's voice yelled. "You stop that!"

Calling the dogs as she ran, Merry reached the beach car just as the startled driver threw back the tarp. The little conscript sat up from its hiding place between bedrolls and food hamper. It stared around, owl-eyed, bewildered, hair in wild disarray. The dogs stood whining, hackles slightly raised. Catching sight of the house, the child's mouth dropped open. Totally enthralled, it rose to its knees and absentmindedly pushed aside the dogs for a better view. "Oh, my!" Merry heard it say. "Oh, my!"

"Careful, Miss Ambrose. Don't get too close," the crewman warned. "Some of these little kids go crazy if they think you're gonna catch them again. They stow away on anything that flies. Creep on board like mice." If the small child heard, it paid no attention, awed by where it found itself.

"Why do they do that?" asked Merry.

"They're homesick. They—sir!" The crewman saluted as the general joined Merry.

"How did this happen?" he asked, half smiling, half annoyed.

At that the child turned and fixed him with a look. "I'm not a *this*. I'm a person," it announced. "My name is Sami Mead, and I'm a girl, and I live in Wheeling!" And then she glanced at Merry and said, "Hi," as if they'd never met.

"I told her to hide here, sir. I said I'd help her get home."

It was impossible to tell what her grandfather was thinking as he studied her face, then looked at the little girl, then again at Merry. "We'd better discuss this privately," he said, and took her arm. "Watch the child, sergeant." The child watched them walk away.

"We can say a mistake was made on test scores," Merry pleaded after she'd told him the whole story. "It probably was. She's very bright. And she offered to help me when she thought I was in trouble. She looked starved, and it's too cold to sleep outside. She might die. . . ."

"She's hidden out for a month next door to the guard station?"

"Yes, sir."

"Determined little thing." He removed the hat he'd been wearing, folded it into a V and tucked the wad behind his belt, took off his sunglasses, polished them and put them in his shirt pocket. The glasses had left a red dent across his nose. The bags beneath his eyes were silky with fatigue.

"Very well. We have to learn the hard way, you and I. She can go home. I'll take care of the details. Until she's in her parents' custody again, you're responsible for her. To avoid offending the staff here, I suggest you take her in through the service entrance. Have the house physician bathe and check her out before you take her near the living quarters."

"Are you angry?"

"I'm not pleased. But at your age, in a similar situation, I'd have made the same mistake—possibly with even less discretion." He paused to find his sunglasses and put them on again. "I've learned that old maxim is true: no good deed goes unpunished. You can be sure, Meredith, that this child will remember you and this place and what her existence might have been long after you've forgotten her. She may never forgive you. Now come. We don't have much time before the others get here." He turned and hurried off, shouting for Williams, who came at a trot and looked harassed.

Merry followed more slowly. Sometimes she didn't understand the things the general said, not even after puzzling them over, but she remembered the gist of his words and, because she respected him, believed they would make sense sometime. But what might she do that this little girl would never forgive? She intended only kindness.

"Where are we?" Sami asked as she followed Merry up the driveway.

"In the country. We'll take you home tomorrow or the next day."

"Oh. Who's the man with whiskers?"

"My grandfather."

"Oh. Is he the boss here?"

"Yes."

"He doesn't wear a uniform." Her tone hinted no one without a uniform could have much authority.

"Usually he does."

"Oh." There was disappointment in that vowel.

They passed the end of the boxwood hedge. Before them lay an avenue of lawn and meadow sloping to the sea. The grass was golden green, the sea beyond milky emerald shading into cobalt. Sami stopped still and stared. "Is that real?" she whispered, and when told it was, she breathed, "Oh, my!" and her eyes got even bigger.

All the house physician said on seeing the child was "You *do* bring me the most interesting patients, Miss Ambrose."

It was odd, Merry thought hours later, when she finally got to take a bath, the difference in people. Sami was as likable as Mikel wasn't. Of course Sami didn't scare her and Mikel did, but it was more than that. She thoughtfully piled up an island of bath bubbles and blew them to the opposite end of the tub. Hot water felt so good after two days without it. She folded her hands behind her head and floated.

The physician had bathed Sami while Merry ran errands for supplies. Sami's knees, feet, and elbows had had to be rubbed with peanut oil to soak off the crusts of grime, her hair cut short to rid it of matted tangles, and even the doctor said she'd never seen toenails in quite that condition. But once the dirt was off, an attractive person emerged, although one much too thin.

Being responsible for someone took a lot of time and effort, but it could also be fun. After Sami's bath they'd given her a pair of Merry's pajamas, the seat of which hung at the girl's knees. A nightshirt wasn't much better; it fit like an ankle-length gown. So while the physical examination was given, Merry rummaged through the wardrobe section of the storerooms, hunting more suitable garments.

The Ambrose family did not believe in waste. In the heyday of the house, clothing had been kept to accommodate all types of guests and occasions; even garments left behind by visitors were stored. No matter that these garments grew old and out of style; quality fabrics lasted far longer than their owners. Some of the clothes collected there were almost as old as the house.

Merry chose several bright silk blouses, green corduroy tights, and a pair of blue wool slacks—which, unknown to her, had been left here by her father on a visit during his childhood. These, some underwear, and two sweaters were the best she could do. She had viewed her choices doubtfully, half embarrassed to offer them to her guest. Besides being out of style, none of these clothes were new and all looked small. Halfway back to the medical suite, she remembered shoes and had to go back to the storeroom.

Sami loved it all. She'd been eating crackers and soup ordered by the doctor—remembering those thick noodles made Merry's stomach growl—and had interrupted herself in spite of her hunger to admire every item. Her genuine pleasure in the things made Merry wonder what the girl's life had been like before conscription.

In the history of the house no commoner had ever occupied a guest room. That strict rule remained unbroken. Sami was put in Worth's old rooms and liked them, perhaps because she didn't know any better. When she stretched out on the bed to "test" it, she fell asleep so quickly that Merry at first couldn't believe she wasn't joking. Then Merry was afraid she'd died, or at least fainted, but the physician, who'd come upstairs with her, said no, "That child's worn out." Merry wasn't sure that was all, because the doctor was still in Sami's bedroom, sitting by the fireplace, reading, and keeping an eye on her. She'd ordered dinner sent up.

In the stillness now construction sounds could be heard from the depths of the house. At nightfall airtrucks had arrived, carrying technicians and equipment to replace what Mikel had destroyed. Two of the trucks would remain here, for the estate.

Lights went on outside and glared off the bathroom window. Curious to know what was happening, Merry sat up abruptly in the bathtub, sending water and suds surging over onto the floor. From the sound of the wind through the trees, another airtruck was coming. By the time she'd rinsed her hair and toweled off, the truck had landed. Wrapped in a thick towel, she hurried out to the lounge to look out through the windows.

A fifth truck had joined the others on the field east of the barns. A small procession of SSF officers was moving slowly up the driveway, carrying a body tightly secured to a stretcher. Merry suddenly shivered, although the room was warm. Mikel was back.

chapter XIII

DINNER WAS A SOLITARY AFFAIR. THE GENERAL WAS "BUSY," Williams told her. She'd rather expected that, and although she missed his company, hunger tempered her disappointment.

She found something quite satisfying about the look of lamb chops; the graceful curve of bone, the plump little oval of meat rimmed with crisp fat. Where the very size of a steak might discourage, lamb chops were always inviting. She ate three, with tiny potatoes, parsleyed and buttered, and a salad vinaigrette, all preceded by a cup of creamy lobster bisque and followed by a flaky apple dumpling, sparkling with cinnamon sugar and served with clotted cream.

Oddly enough, she didn't feel sleepy after dinner, merely restless. On her way upstairs she roamed through the main salons. The rooms were still, their lights on, their windows reflecting back the emptiness—like an elegant museum, she thought, complete with paintings and cut flowers and grand pianos never played but kept in perfect tune.

The doctor had fallen asleep in the chair, book open on her

lap. A breeze from the window ruffled the pages. Sami was curled like a kitten beneath a yellow wool blanket, so soundly asleep that her body scarcely moved with breathing. Safe for now, Merry thought, looking down at her and wondering again how she'd lived a month in that debris, with rain and cold and rotten food and no bathroom—and had escaped pneumonia at the very least. Merry tried to imagine doing that and decided she could if she had to. But why would anyone feel that they had to?

The bedroom was cold, and as she went to shut the window, she glanced out and saw a round green glow. One of the domes in the oldest, most dilapidated wing of the house was lit. Had they taken Mikel there? Or were some of the electronics technicians searching for old hookups? She quietly shut the window, covered the doctor, book and all, with a blanket, and tiptoed from the suite. She would go for a walk before bedtime.

She knew she'd get lost if she tried to find her way to that dome through the halls, but if one knew how to follow the twists and turns, a pathway of pounded sand connected all the gardens and eventually circled the entire house, wandering in among the wings and out again. She'd followed it one summer evening just for the fun of it. You turned left across the front portico and kept on walking.

There were few driveway or garden lamps at the north end of the house. A pine grove planted as a windbreak had grown so tall that the trees shut out even starlight. Now that she was near to where the lighted dome should be, there was no sign of it, but then, she reasoned, it might be a courtyard dome hidden by walls unless one looked down on it from a higher point. Several times she left the path to try doors but found them either locked or bricked shut. In one alcove she tripped over a raccoon. They gave each other a bad scare. She yelled, it snarled, and both frantically scrambled away. There were other animals running over the leaves. Perhaps the raccoon had young ones?

115

Then from close by came the sound of singing, a clear, sweet voice, a capella in an almost ritual chant. Or was it a computer? The tone was flawlessly pure. She hurried down the path and around a corner. A large square of pink light framed a pine bough. Two SSF officers stepped out of the light, and the door closed. The singing stopped. She edged behind a tree as they approached, their boots crunching in the sand.

"He's kept this up for an hour now," one man said.

"Does he know what he's doing?" the other asked.

"The psychiatrist says no, that he's repeating a programmed . . ." The wind sighed through the pines, and the words were lost.

". . . comes from space? He's an alien?"

". . . not sure he's human."

"He's human—that's what the computer says. And I for one don't believe that story about the moon." The man laughed. "Just because there are no records on him?" Their voices faded into the night.

The door was wide enough to admit a small car and had a ramp instead of a sill, as if it were a delivery entrance. When she opened the door, she found a wide pink marble hall, empty but for life-size nude statues at intervals around the walls. There was a hazy golden door at the far end and an open archway in the center of the right-hand wall. A cold breeze swept past, smelling of old perfumes. The singing was much louder here in this boxed space, a pleasant sound, inviting in its wordless purity.

She closed the door quickly, crossed over to the arch, and found the dome she'd been hunting. It covered a lawn, lush and emerald-green under hidden lighting. Set flat into the grass were marble slabs with gold lettering. In the left wall of the archway a smaller arch opened onto a marble staircase leading down into darkness. The perfume scent drifted up that stairwell.

"It's a mausoleum!" she whispered aloud. The idea gave her goose bumps, and she shivered, then immediately felt silly. Why should that scare her? Still . . . she took two deep breaths and exhaled slowly each time to relax.

"Meredith?" She jumped several inches off the floor when her grandfather touched her shoulder. "I'm sorry," he apologized. "I should have realized you couldn't hear me over the music." He took her arm to steady her. "We saw you come in. The gold door's one-way glass. I take it you're curious about the boy?"

The general was in uniform again. Obviously one of the airtrucks had brought along clothing for him. He looked more familiar to her now and at the same time more distant.

"Why did you bring him down here?"

"It seemed the perfect place to—uh—interview him. If he gets the urge to burn anything, this wing is fireproof. Also remote from the rest of the house."

"Is *he* singing?"

"Strange, isn't it? As if a three-year-old could not only sing but remember a marvelously complex aria. We're recording it. We haven't the vaguest idea what it's about or why he's doing it. You see, with a bit of chemical assistance and a few kind words, a psychiatrist has regressed him to three years of age— or claims to have done so. This song is the result. We're about to urge him forward. Would you like to be present?"

She hesitated. "Is Avril Otabai buried here?"

His eyes became vague for a moment. "Not in here. She's on the hill. Only the oldest are here." His lips narrowed in a humorless smile. "When this was built, funeral customs were a bit extreme. You've never been in here before?" She shook her head. "Then it's nothing to see at night. These memorial statues are bad enough. They were carved by computer, you know, using the subject as a template. Come. I must get back."

There was an old laboratory behind that gold door, much to her surprise. The room was equipped with sinks and tanks and two long, narrow tables. Other, much newer equipment stood on metal carts. She couldn't imagine why a lab should be here, and with strangers present, she didn't want to ask. General Ambrose introduced her to three doctors, a professor, and several high-ranking SSF officers—none of whose names she remembered for more than seconds for staring at Mikel.

Wrapped in a pink sheet, he lay in what appeared to be a large wide-mouth glass jar, set on a pedestaled cradle designed for that purpose. Tubes and wires led inside, some disappearing beneath the sheet. A small microphone and speaker were stuck to the glass above his head. He looked as if he were singing in his sleep. His face looked thinner, as if he'd lost weight.

"Where did you get that?" she asked, referring to the jar.

"It's a rather lucky find, don't you think?" the general said. "A proper container for the thing contained?"

"We're ready," a doctor said. "If you'll be seated, please. Out of the light. The patient's eyes may open, and we want nothing to distract him or make him aware of externals." The woman paused, looked at Merry, then told the general, "Sir, I must warn you that this drug blocks the inhibitors. The results may be embarrassing or uncomfortable for your granddaughter."

"If he becomes gross, we'll be the first to leave," he assured her. "Don't waste time with nonessentials. I want basic facts— where's he from, who his parents are, what he came here to do. Bring him up to an age where he can hold a sensible conversation."

As she climbed onto a lab stool behind a long marble-topped table, Merry saw Mikel's body jerk as though he'd received an electric shock. He stopped singing, stirred restlessly, and turned his head from side to side, then began to fret as a baby does when frightened half-awake by fear or pain. She paused, one foot still on the floor, not sure she wanted to stay and watch this. Whatever he was, he was helpless and outnumbered now, and her sense of fair play objected.

"Is he responding to the drug so quickly?" the general asked.

"No. It hasn't been administered yet—"

"And if you try I'll burst this bubble into a million pieces." Mikel's sweet voice filled the room so completely that it was obvious he'd been singing almost under his breath. "You'll all be killed."

SSF officers moved to shield the general, weapons ready. The doctors and the professor dropped to the floor. Only Merry failed to move. Afterward she thought she'd been stupid, but at the time she was afraid only that she'd miss something by hiding on the floor. When the room was quiet again, the general said, "Very well. Blow it up." His human shield stirred uneasily.

The boy's head turned to find the speaker outside his crystal prison. He squinted against the overhead light.

"I'm waiting, Mikel . . . but before you try, I suggest you notice that you're wrapped in full body restraints. You can't run from any fire or even free your arms."

Mikel lay still, staring out at a point near the general, then tried to move his arms and legs, his face twisting with the effort. The covering sheet moved only slightly.

"Be careful now," the general warned. "Don't hurt yourself. We don't know how to treat the type of burns you inflict. You'd die in agony. That would be unfortunate." His tone said it wouldn't bother him a bit.

The boy stopped squirming. Merry saw him take a deep breath and exhale slowly, then another, deeper breath, and he began to scream, a brilliantly loud E above high C—which he held for what seemed forever, only to slide into a series of shorter, sharper notes that made his audience automatically cover their ears, and metal items in the room vibrate. The jar didn't even tremble.

He stopped as shortly as he'd started when a thin trickle of blood ran from his nose.

"Very good!" The general consulted the clock. "You held that first note forty-two seconds. Very impressive. It's too bad the trapped sound gave you a nosebleed. You could have an outstanding career in opera, although I would imagine the number of lyric tenor roles is limited in our age. Now, to save time—the vessel you're in is unbreakable, as are your restraints. Shall we go ahead and get this awkward interview over with? You're obviously a member of a very elite corps or you wouldn't be here."

With his left hand, which was hidden by the sturdy figure of the SSF man in front of him, the general was signaling to the psychiatrist still crouched behind a sink. The psychiatrist rose cautiously until she could see the portable terminal on the sink top, reached up, and touched three buttons. One of the fine tubes running into the jar turned pink as the general went on talking. ". . . an elite corps, trained from childhood to do extraordinary things, things no person on Earth could ever hope to do . . ." His voice lulled on and on. Mikel's gaze wavered and became fixed.

Almost on cue, Merry thought as she leaned on her elbows and watched. Is the drug working, or is he smart enough to know he's being given more drugs and he's pretending it's working? she wondered. If he'd told her the truth, that he could *make molecules dance* to convert them into energy—whatever that meant to him—could he possibly recognize the chemicals entering his system and break them down or block their receptors? Could the mind be trained to do that?

The door slid open, and she glanced around, expecting to see the two officers she'd seen on the path. Then she gave an involuntary "oh!" of surprise that made heads turn. It was Sami, barefoot, dressed only in her long pink nightshirt, looking breathless and bewildered. After the briefest glance around the room, she headed straight toward the glass jar.

Merry and an SSF captain caught her, one by each arm, and she tried to tug away. "No!" Merry whispered, and the smaller girl looked up at her, at first frightened, then relieved as she saw who it was.

"Is this the place?" she whispered. "It didn't sound like this at all. It sounded beautiful and important. . . ." She tried to see around the general's little group and, failing that, crouched down and looked through their legs. "That's him in there, isn't it? The one who called us? When he stopped, I got scared again. It's so dark in some of those halls. I just found this room by accident."

"Get her out of here! Outside! She's disturbing him!" the psychiatrist hissed. Merry glanced at Mikel, who was smiling beautifully, and at her grandfather, who nodded, frowning.

The captain picked up Sami and carried her out into the hall, Merry at his heels. "She must have followed me," Merry said as the door closed behind them. "She was sound asleep."

"I've a son who sleepwalks," the officer said, "but if you talk to him while he's doing it, you'd swear he was awake—until he says something about the dream he's in at the moment."

"I'm awake," said Sami. "He woke me up."

"You must be freezing, barefoot on this stone floor. Here—" Merry sat down, pulled off her boots, and gave the little girl her cashmere socks, then put her jacket over Sami's shoulders as Sami pulled on the footwear. "How did you follow me in the dark—and barefoot?"

"Did he call you, too?"

"No."

Sami stared up at her, then gave the gold door a look that plainly said she'd like to talk, if only to be polite, but not now. There was something else she must do now.

"You can't go in there again," the captain said. "You have to go to bed."

She turned her back on him. "I didn't go outside. I came here through the building," she told Merry. "It's awful big and empty. Is it an old hotel like in pictures?"

"Something like that," Merry said, trying to understand. "How did you find your way?"

"I don't know," she said shyly. "Just walked. It's scary. Why is he inside a glass like the people downstairs? Are they real?"

"What?"

"The beautiful man. Why is he in a jar like the people down there?" She pointed to the stairwell in the arch. "I thought they were dead because they're so still, but maybe they're only sleeping." She frowned, then shivered. "Their jars have lids. How do they breathe? They can't be real . . . can they?"

Merry and the SSF officer exchanged glances, but before either could say anything the courtyard door opened and the two men she'd seen on the path came in. They had trouble closing the door because of Bo and Bernie. Both dogs were trying to come in, and as the door shut they began to bark in protest. Their behavior struck her as odd; the dogs never came up to the house, and after her bath they couldn't be tracking Sami.

"It's the funniest thing," one man called as he paused to brush dog hair off his trousers, "but there's a bunch of deer, a goat, sheep, and a lot of little animals out there milling around in the dark like they were expecting to be fed or something. They weren't there when we went out. It's weird."

"Maybe he called them, too?" Sami said shyly.

"Who called who? Who's the kid?"

"She's a sleepwalker," the captain said. "She's going back to bed."

"I'm not sleepwalking!" Sami objected. "He called me. He

needed help . . . he promised . . ." She saw them all looking at her and went quiet with shyness.

"You mean the man who sings?" Merry asked softly, and Sami nodded. "Can you hear him now?" Sami shook her head. "But when you did, he *promised*—the song promised?" Again came a nod. Merry took a deep breath. "What did he promise?"

"He said a shepherd moon would take care of us, that we wouldn't be lonely or afraid. I don't know what that means, but it sounded nice. What's a shepherd?"

"Maybe he'll explain in the morning," Merry said, feeling rather unreal herself, "but you have to go back to bed now and get warm. Your doctor's probably worried—"

"She's sleeping."

"Lieutenant." The captain summoned one of the men. "You two escort her back to the house proper. Miss Ambrose will give you directions. Personally see to it that the child's tucked in to stay."

"Can I come back here in the morning?" Sami asked Merry.

"We'll talk about it then. Now promise me you won't go anywhere else alone until you talk to me. You could get lost in this building. Promise?"

"I can take care of myself."

"I know," Merry said gently, "but promise?"

"I promise," Sami said, but with great reluctance.

"Is she a cousin?" the captain asked as the door closed on the trio, Sami being carried piggyback to protect her feet.

"No," Merry said, but didn't explain. She was staring at the far door. How would Sami know about a shepherd moon? She couldn't have heard him singing—and yet apparently she had, just as she had found her way here through what must have been a labyrinth of halls—or else the night outside. But if that song called to Sami, why hadn't anyone else responded? Then she remembered the animals. Perhaps only animals and young children had ears sensitive enough to hear whatever it was, like a dog whistle.

"Miss Ambrose?" The captain's gesture was an invitation to precede him back into the lab.

"In a little while. I'm going to check something downstairs."

"Shall I go with you?"

She hesitated, wanting to say yes, but knowing instinctively her grandfather wouldn't like to have a stranger down there. "No, thank you. That won't be necessary."

Going down those steps was like descending into a cold deep dry well. She missed her jacket. Six steps down an automatic switch turned on lights and revealed a trail of bare footprints on the dust—one small print per step leading up. Sami had climbed these stairs. At the bottom was a tiny lobby. The high arch of its entrance framed lush greenery. It was as if she were walking into a cold terrarium lit by an evening sun.

chapter XIV

HERE, IN FORMAL DRESS, AS IF SLEEP HAD OVERWHELMED them in a garden after a ball, were almost two dozen people, each perfectly preserved in a clear container, irradiated, vacuum-sealed. Their beds looked like green velvet. Their pillows were white satin. No one looked old, but none was young. Pearls glowed on waxen ears; gold braid and buttons gleamed. Here and there a gentle smile suggested pleasant dreams.

The favored spot seemed to be a knoll beneath a trio of white birches. When Merry paused beside a tomb, a key light came on, focused on the face. Beside each was an identifying pedestal column, with a screen, and buttons one could touch to view and hear a biography, moments of their life encapsulated with them. The latest date on a pedestal was more than two hundred years old.

From speakers hidden in the leaf canopy came birdsong. Flowers bloomed in unexpected places. Fish swam in lighted pools. All was serene as moss.

As she followed the flagstone pathway that wound among the

trees, she glanced at the still faces. This probably was how the old story of Snow White got started, she thought. Perhaps all of them had a bite of the Wicked Queen's apple lodged in their throat? With a kiss and a pat on the back they might walk again.

The path came out on a wide-bricked open area. Beyond were bronze doors dark with age, and a brushed metal door, still shiny, obviously to a freight elevator. With effort, she pushed open one of the bronze doors. Light came on in the empty corridor, where, beside one wall, a trail of childish footprints led to this door and entered, to disappear on the gray brick. Sami had found her way here through the house.

As the weight of the door pushed her back in closing, Merry glimpsed part of the engraving on the doorfront: "immortal" and "forever" below it, and she wondered what that had meant to these ancestors of hers. Did they believe that somehow, sometime, for those with enough wealth and power, there would be an antidote for death, and when that time came, they would be ready? She shivered then, and not with cold.

Suddenly she could not face the thought of retracing her way through that room and back up those winding stairs. She touched the elevator button, guessing that the lift could have carried only one kind of freight down here. There was a hiss, a quiet creaking in the wall, and the big door slid open.

Moments later she stepped out into a service room full of strange equipment and old chemical smells. A faded red door said: DANGER—RADIATION, a worn blue LAB/PREP. Stacked along one wall, like empty bottles in a wine rack, were six more containers, dusty enough to have held vintage years. A seventh slot was empty, the dust around it recently disturbed.

Heads turned as she entered the lab. Mikel seemed to be telling a story, his voice the only sound in the room. As she tiptoed around the table to take her original seat, her grandfather gave her a questioning glance. She nodded. He shook his head in resignation as if to say, "It's done now, but I wish you hadn't seen that." Some time passed before her pulse returned to normal and she could settle down and listen.

What the boy was saying now seemed oddly familiar. She'd heard it all before. "That's from an old space opera!" she blurted aloud, suddenly remembering. "*Orphan from Orion*—it's in the entertainment archives here—or was, before he melted things." As she sketched the plot, she was interrupted by laughter that went on and on. Mikel was apparently quite pleased by his elaborate joke.

"Why didn't the drug work?" The general's question evoked some hemming and hawing from the medical staff.

"We're dealing with a psychotic per—"

"You out there!" Mikel shouted into the microphone just above his head. "Your drugs are useless. I've been trained to neutralize any harmful substance I'm given! If you want to talk to me, you must recognize my superiority. I'll tell you what you want to know—when I'm free of this thing I'm in."

The general reached over and turned off Mikel's microphone. "Could anyone be trained to neutralize a drug?" he asked the medical quartet. After some debate they decided it was highly improbable. "Yet he did it."

"Not necessarily, sir. The chemistry of the psychotic mind isn't fully understood. It's possible that extreme stress would produce in the patient an extraordinarily high drug tolerance. I've seen patients—"

"You don't *know* he is insane. He may be a perfectly normal citizen of Terra II."

Merry saw that remark made them all avert their eyes, clear their throats uneasily, and straighten uniform sleeves. They didn't believe Mikel came from Terra II. Moreover, they were embarrassed that the general might think otherwise. Mikel was making her grandfather look a fool. But then Mikel had made her look ungracious and a liar.

She wasn't by nature vengeful or given much to anger, perhaps because her life had so far been pleasant—but to see her grandfather thought bonkers by members of his staff angered her. Leaving the adults still debating, she slid off the stool, picked up the general's mike, walked over to the jar, and rapped sharply on its surface.

"Do you know what you're in?" she asked as his beautiful eyes focused on her face. "You're in a tomb. That's what we do with dead people here—put them in a jar, put on the lid, vacuum-seal it, irradiate the package to kill bacteria, and store it in a special room where people can come and see you for always. That's what we're going to do with you. You'll be preserved forever. Canned goods. Isn't that nice?"

For the first time she saw uncertainty flicker on his face. Encouraged, she went on. "There are lots of containers like this downstairs. When you join them, you'll look as if you fell asleep on the grass, with glass over you to keep off bugs and dust. And you'll always be as pretty as you are tonight. Prettier, probably. We'll dress you in the yellow suit you came in. . . ." She gazed off into the distance thoughtfully. "Since we don't know much about you—except that you're a killer—we could add a recording of your song to the monument. You'll be a dead Pied Piper. I always wondered where he took the children. Where do you take them?"

He spoke then. She could see his lips move but couldn't hear what he said. She stepped away to turn the jar mike back on. It was the best move she could have made; her going left him prey to his imagination.

They didn't care that he was superior. They were going to kill him! Like Worth when she saw what he'd done to her friends. Stupid Worth—she thought he wouldn't guess she intended to sacrifice herself by delivering him to what she called medical authorities. She thought she was smart enough and strong enough to control *him*. It was fortunate for him she had such misguided self-confidence. Had she been smarter and properly afraid, she would have shot him. That might have been better. To die in a vacuum? As if he were in space? The girl was cruel to think of that.

Why didn't they come when he called them? Why did no one respond? That was when his fear began, when he sang for Worth. Only things she called coyotes answered, and four village children who stared up at him with big dark eyes and had no image to respond to. While he was trying to understand what had gone wrong, Worth's friends grew angry and accused her of jeopardizing all of them by bringing in a madman. He'd visited them as they slept, and touched them, one by one.

She stood outside the glass again, that girl he should have killed, staring at him, gloating. "Did Worth and her friends decide you were more danger than help? Maybe sound works differently on Earth? Did you think of that? Suppose it's like a dog whistle here—only certain ears can hear your promises? How does it work on Terra II?"

In spite of his anger, part of what she said made sense. They heard the summons but were able to ignore it. That was a frightening thought. As primitive as they were, perhaps they'd never been programmed? Programming had to begin at birth while the cells were still receptive and response patterns could be fixed. Once certain receptors began to atrophy, the loss was irreversible, the mind forever lost to control. If that was the norm here, he was in desperate trouble.

The trick now was to stall for time until he could find a way out of this trap. The best way to do that would be to give them what they thought they wanted. He would proceed in careful stages.

It seemed to Merry that his face began to pale. In seconds he looked ill and defeated. "You can kill me," he said, his voice soft and clear with despair. "It doesn't matter now. They know I reached Earth safely. They can follow. You can't stop them. They know I survived the landing."

"How would they know?" she asked. "Can you talk with Terra II?"

His answer was no help. "The signal stops with brain death."

"Why were you sent here? Why did you kill the others?"

He began to talk then as if he couldn't stop, as if by finally obeying their wishes he could delay his death. Much of what he said made no sense to them, not because he babbled but because he spoke of a life so different that they couldn't imagine it. It was as if someone from the twentieth century spoke to people of the sixteenth.

He used words that had no meaning, and other words that couldn't be understood within the context of his speech: Klebermine, sterile breeder, dry rain, gravlac. But he didn't admit killing his companions. "They will come," he kept repeating. "They will build shuttles, and they will come. All the executive committee, all the teaching stewards, all the guards—all will come. Seven million to a moon. Less but never more." At times he lapsed into foreign speech or sang a word or phrase.

All their questions were ignored. He didn't appear to hear them but talked through their attempts to interrupt. As time went on he seemed less and less aware of externals, drugged now by the sound of his voice. An hour passed, then two. The SSF officers began to get restless, whispering among themselves, ignoring the glares of the psychiatrist.

At one a.m. her grandfather leaned close and whispered, "You must go to bed." Only cold and perverse pride were keeping her awake. Her eyes burned, and she'd been swallowing yawns for more than an hour. Mikel was still talking as she left the room. Several of the SSF officers looked at her enviously.

A brisk wind had risen. The stars were clear and close. There were no animals in the courtyard, but a deer leaped over the path a few yards out. Lights still burned in the occupied part of the house, as they would until the general had gone to bed. Movement and the wind revived her, and she hurried along, arms hugging her chest for warmth, almost running, lost in thought.

The only person he talked about was someone called the Master. He never mentioned parents. From what little she understood he had no family or friends. Because he had been in some way a special baby, he'd been trained by machines, computers of some sort that sang and showed him endless pictures. "Reality, not symbols," he'd kept repeating. "Liquid, solid, gas. Gas, liquid, solid. Bond, unbond. Never burn. Destroy only to create. Preserve the balance always. Preserve the beauty and the space."

She thought he'd been made a medical officer of some sort because he said, "With my voice I make them docile and unafraid. With my hands I can heal anyone I touch or release them to redistribution. I can outwit the tribelong, outsing a mamatron, make them love The Shepherd Moon." But he didn't say what that meant. Of course, were their positions reversed, where would she begin to tell his people what her world was like?

In a way the world he talked about reminded her of that room downstairs, coldly beautiful, full of systems and facades designed to hide lifelessness. Terra II seemed a place where things had been preserved so long they had become unwholesome.

She shuddered with cold and began to run. What if his people did come here? Where would they live? What would they eat? And were they all like Mikel? It didn't seem fair somehow that what was done centuries ago should echo now in her lifetime and have to be dealt with.

If her parents had come home when they'd promised to, she

would have been in school and wouldn't have had to know about or be scared by this. And she wouldn't know about conscripted children or ugly flyover towns, and Worth would be alive. Even though she didn't like her, Merry was sorry Worth was dead. But then, she thought, I would have missed seeing the moons and that fire in the sky, and the time with the general, and Sami would be sleeping in that filthy ruin. And unpleasant as some of it was, it was also the most interesting time she'd ever spent. So she couldn't wish it hadn't happened.

Slowing to a trot, out of breath as well as confused, she was startled by a window opening in the wall looming beside her. A white head poked out, a shadowed face stared down—an old and pensioned servant wondering who was running in the garden after midnight, frightened or indignant at this unusual disturbance.

She gave a little laugh as understanding struck. If you were of her class, it could all be ignored—anything unpleasant. Her parents did that; in his own way, so did her grandfather—he could mourn a bronze soldier but not a dead officer. Her ancestors had tried to ignore dying. Her great-grandmother had apparently decided to ignore the entire world. But the world went on, waiting to be dealt with, if not now, later. And if she cared about herself, she'd have to learn to deal with it. It was a question not of power but of responsibility; someone had to take it. Otherwise things went on coasting into ruin.

As she crossed the flagstones by the side door, a falling star slashed the sky high overhead. A wave drowned the beach in an enormous rush and receded into quiet.

Sami was snoring, arms around a pillow. Beside her lay the house doctor, cocooned in a plaid comforter, still guarding in her sleep. Merry stood for a moment watching, listening to those cozy sleeping sounds. As she turned away, her face bore a look of wistfulness.

chapter XV

HE WAS EXHAUSTED, BUT HE WENT ON TALKING LONG AFTER he saw her leave the room, long enough to guess she wouldn't return. Those adult shadows out there, each preoccupied by self-importance, by dominance in their own narrow little worlds, all underestimated him or dismissed him as a fraud. From their stupid questions, they hoped to gain knowledge from him that would add to their own power.

But the girl knew; he was sure now. She had found his pose tiresome and had gone to bed. She must be very powerful or they wouldn't have brought him back to where she was. She had slapped him once for acting. If he'd tried in her presence what he was about to do, she probably would have ordered the lid put on him and personally turned on the compressor.

What a disgusting idea! Barbaric! Preserved bodies!

He began to stutter, to slur his speech, to be silent for long intervals. His breathing became labored and he coughed, softly at first to get their full attention, then violently as if choking. He slowed his pulse, arched his back as much as possible, and went limp, eyes rolled back in extremis.

Furniture scraped on the stone floor. Footsteps approached. There were inquiring murmurs and several quick commands. The pallet on which he lay was moved, and his head emerged into cooler, sweeter air. Hands touched the wrappings on his shoulders, and he was hurriedly unbound. He allowed himself a glimpse of chins and necks bending over him—some with facial hair and enlarged pores. He let his eyelids close. His eyes hurt from rolling them up like that.

They lay him on a table and unstrapped his arms. Cold hands and instruments touched his bare chest. Only discipline controlled involuntary response.

"He seems to be dying, General."

"Shoot him if he tries to touch anyone!"

"You don't mean that, surely?"

"I've seen his victims. The order stands."

It might be best to go into deep sleep now and let them do what they would. Sleep would lull them, and he needed rest. Setting his internal timing system, he retreated.

Cold through when she reached her rooms, Merry took a hot bath before going to bed. She was just drifting off when she heard footsteps in the service hall. The now-empty study served as a sounding box, picking up the knock on Sami's door and the mumble of voices.

". . . can't get him to wake up," a man's voice said. "You know the most about him."

" . . . wasn't eating . . ." the doctor said. "I'll be right with you."

Someone must be sick and they've sent for the doctor, she thought dopily, as she heard two pairs of footsteps hurry away. She snuggled down in the pillows and then sat up. That meant Sami was alone, probably asleep, but still her responsibility. Yawning, she got up, put on her robe and slippers, and went across the hall to check.

Sami was asleep and gave no indication of waking soon. Merry looked out the window to where the far dome still glowed green. Maybe he would talk all night? She yawned again. That empty half of Sami's bed looked tempting, but she didn't like the idea of sleeping so close to a stranger. Besides, she'd stay only until the doctor returned. Taking the comforter, she curled up in the lounge chair. You can hardly hear the sea in here, was her last waking thought.

Vaguely unpleasant dreams twisted through her mind. Once she woke crying but couldn't remember why. The doctor hadn't returned. Drifting back to sleep again, she dreamed her mother was dancing with Mikel. Both had shiny yellow clothes and golden hair, but Mikel was the prettier, and her mother told him indignantly, "I'll never stand beside you for a picture. You dim my radiance. It's all we have, you know." A door opened and they danced away into the fog. A door closed. Footsteps ran away.

She opened her eyes, half awake, saw the doctor had returned and was asleep again, and let her eyes fall shut. How could anyone get to bed and back to sleep that fast? She sat up. The doctor was alone in the bed. She checked the lounge and bathroom. Sami was gone.

He woke in a room smelly with medicinals and a faint layer of human breath. He could hear no monitoring devices. Two people close by were slowly breathing as if in sleep. He opened his eyes just enough to peer beneath the lids. He was reclining on a contour lounge, naked beneath a blanket, his left arm secured to a cradle so that a hollow needle could drip liquid into a vein. They were feeding him! He could taste the salty sweetness in his mouth. What an odd way to do it—and after they'd pretended not to have decent food. Liars. Stupid liars.

To the right and left of his lounge, guards slumped in chairs.

Both men slept open-mouthed, heads fallen back, guns cradled against their stomachs. From their carelessness he assumed they expected him to die without regaining consciousness. His ruse had worked. His smile was beautiful.

It took him several minutes to free his wrists and ankles from the shackles and detach the chain belt from his waist. It took him that long because he was careful not to make a sound or burn himself with the chain links. He removed the IV needle and sterile-sealed the puncture wound, drank the remaining liquid, saw two more paks waiting to be hung, and drank those before stealthily getting up.

There was no time to waste in attempting conversion of these men. Besides, the smell might attract others. A quick, hard pinch at the base of their skulls and the guards now needed assistance before they could ever wake again. He put the smaller of the two on the lounge and left in the man's uniform, carrying both weapons. Digital numbers above the hatch read 5:05 a.m. He thought it was a traffic counter; as he opened the hatch the number changed to 5:06.

A guard in the corridor turned and looked at him as Mikel reached for the guard's neck. The man slid down the wall and toppled sideways. Mikel put out his foot to keep the head from striking the floor with a warning *clunk*.

The corridor was empty. He sidled along one wall, unnerved by the cold silence, the dust and dimness. He was free now, but where could he go? Where were there people among whom he could hide?

He opened a hatch and slipped through into a cold, dark room. That room led to another, and another, all empty, all decaying. Soon he felt as lost and alone as if he'd been exiled again to an abandoned section. They had done that once, when he was small, sent him away to endure or die, to learn what fear felt like, to teach him why he must never let those he summoned feel fear.

He was surprised that he could remember that. Deep sleep and drug residues must have aroused old imprints. But what was worse, he couldn't block the memory, and it began to overwhelm him.

Alone! Alone and nothing! No one knew! No one cared! He had survived and no one cared! He had survived for nothing! They never told him how big Earth was. They never said how empty. He had been good. And they had wasted him! Wasted him!

He sank down in a dusty anteroom and began to keen, an eerie wailing cry pitched far above most human ears.

Merry paused in the hallway, not knowing which way to go, and called, "Sami?" An answer came, not from her rooms but from far down the service hall. "Come on!"

She caught a glimpse of the little girl on the turn of the service ramp. Sami was still wearing the cashmere socks and jacket Merry had given her. "Sami! Wait up!" She couldn't hear any footsteps.

"We've got to help him!" Sami called. "He's lost and scared!"

"Sami! You promised!"

"This is different. Come on!"

And Sami would not stop. She went straight down the service ramp into the basement level, past the wine cellar and across between the curing rooms. The air here smelled like cheese, and somewhere there were apples. She passed a freight lift labeled "Surface Only," turned left into a passageway and then left again, her route marked by the lights and doors activated by her passing.

Merry tried to keep up, or at least at a respectable distance, but running in slippers and bathrobe was awkward and Sami was much faster. By the time she reached a ramp back to ground floor level, she'd quit wondering how Sami knew where she was going or even why. Not being left behind was the best Merry could manage. Her sides were beginning to ache, and her ears;

the left ear, especially, hurt. When she passed an open window, a dog's howl made her wince.

"Sami! Slow down!"

"You catch up!"

"I can't!"

"Meet you there!"

"You can't see him, Sami!" There was no answer. "Sami? Come back! You can't see Mikel!" She didn't know how or what he was doing, but she was sure it was he who pulled them through this place like a beacon.

They went up another ramp. Here the lights were almost gone, and Merry realized they were in the oldest part of the house. A dimly blinking yellow lamp far down a corridor revealed Sami still running. She leaped a hurdle and went on. The chain, Merry thought, the chain with the danger sign on it. She slowed to gain enough air to call, "Don't go down there! It's not safe!"

But Sami ran on into the darkness. By the time Merry reached that point, she had to step over the chain, clutching her side with one hand, her left ear with the other. There was light in a doorway ahead, and she looked in on the old apartment that had never been disturbed, where the monkey skeleton lay in the tub. She called, got no reply, and went in cautiously.

There was no one there, but when she looked in that bathroom the skeleton was gone, as was the jade necklace that had been entangled with the bones. Mingled with her original tracks in the sand around the tub were the bootprints of one man, and a palm print, as if he'd braced himself on the tub's rim while reaching down. The sand at the bottom of the tub had been raked smooth.

There was no time to puzzle over it. She ran back to the hall. The pain in her ear quit abruptly. Both ears popped as if from altitude. There was a drumming noise. For a moment she wasn't sure if it was real or inside her head. "Sami?"

"This door's stuck!" came the complaint. "He's in there!"

"Don't open it! I'm coming! This part of the house—"

A loud crack like a giant bone breaking silenced her warning. Somewhere a door slid open, screeching on gritty runners. The floor beneath her feet shivered, then shook violently. She froze, unsure which way to run. Glass fell somewhere outside, tinkling and smashing. The floor shook again and lurched right, then left. She was thrown against a wall. There was a smell of dusty sand. Suddenly her feet went out from under her as the floor dropped. For one startled moment she saw a patch of starry sky where no sky should be. A wall rose up, and she was sliding backward, faster, into dusty blackness.

He heard shouts and then someone pounding on a hatch. They'd come to get him! They'd come to take him back! He would be safe again, and needed, and warm. He glowed with relief. Just as he stood, he heard the outer hull warp with that strange noise empty compartments made. But he wasn't frightened, not anymore. They'd come for him! They'd take him into the light.

And then the hatch opened, but instead of a Master, he saw one ugly Earth child staring up at him, open-mouthed and terrified. Beyond was a passageway, barely lit but enough for him to see and remember where he was. They hadn't come.

The madness that began long ago, crooned into him by mamatrons, overwhelmed him now with rage. How dare a child respond when he needed to be saved! He reached out to touch the stranger, and in the dimness cold green energy glowed from him and flowed between his hands. Against its will the child reached out—then squealed and ran. He felt the floor quake and thought it was his will that threw him after the fleeing child just as the I-beam hit him.

Mingled dust of mortar, sand, and plaster poured down over his body as gravity pushed it down into the pile. For a few seconds the dust glowed a faint green, then faded.

During the Three Shift on Terra II, in the core laboratory a pulsating blue light on a monitor screen stopped blinking, glowed steadily for two minutes and eleven seconds, and went out. The last of the cadets sent to Earth was dead. No one noticed for three hours.

chapter XVI

SHE DROPPED THROUGH SPACE, AN ODDLY GIDDY FEELING, felt her slippers fall and felt cold air between her toes. Her robe flew up and flapped over her face. She landed on a lumpy sofa which made a cracking noise, tipped, and sent her rolling to smack painfully full-length against wood. There was a crash directly overhead, and debris rained down. Instinctively she curled up and tried to bury her head in her arms for protection, but her mind said calmly, "You're going to die"—as if her mind were a separate thing observing it all.

Grinding, tearing sounds subsided into individual crashes, as if furniture were falling from upper floors. Something hit her leg, bounced off, and slid away. Silence returned.

She dared to breathe and choked. It was so dark she couldn't see. When she finally managed a few shallow breaths without choking on dust, she tried to sit up but couldn't. There was something right above her back. She could turn onto her back and raise her head about eight inches, but her feet touched solid resistance behind her, and when she tried to worm forward, her fingers struck jumbled bricks. She tried pushing them away and heard the pile start to slip and stopped, afraid something more might fall.

"Sami?" she called. "Sami?" and then forced herself not to cough for several seconds while waiting for an answer. None came.

She was trapped.

She had been too surprised to be afraid before, but as the thought of being trapped sank in, all the threat, all the fear of the last few weeks came back in one terrible rush. Her heart began to pound, her stomach churned, and she retched and kept on retching until there was nothing left to throw up. Completely miserable, she began to cry and found crying hurt as much as throwing up.

Why didn't they fix this place or tear it down instead of leaving it to fall? Why didn't they care—why didn't anyone care? Why did Sami have to run away? She'd promised! And now Sami was probably dead as well as Mikel. It seemed unfair that all of them had come so far just to die in this ruin. Self-pity faded as her crying washed away some of her shock.

She sniffed, and the disgusting whiff made her remember her first glimpse of Mikel. He had been sick inside that thing and he was crying . . . and she could begin to understand why and even pity him. It must have been a terrible trip, trapped in there. No wonder he was crazy. Whatever he was or had been, he hadn't gotten that way all by himself. He'd been trained—or perverted—to serve someone else's purposes. What sort of people would do things like that? But then . . . what sort of people would conscript Sami? Or tell Worth she was an orphan?

And then it all came clear. The danger was not Mikel or his Shepherd Moon, but her world, her people, and what they had become. Mikel was like the meteoroid, a stray bit of the past altered by time into something lethal should it accidentally cross one's path. That he had crossed theirs was random chance, but to Worth he had been a chance worth taking—to change her world—a very different world from Merry's. Worth was dead, but there must be a million Worths—Sami could become one if she was still alive. How long would it take before Sami learned to hate as Worth had hated?

Suppose she, Merry, had been born in Sami's place and Sami born in hers?

Merry stared off into that imagined future, focusing on a crack of pale blue light. Her grandfather said to accept, to be glad. But she wasn't sure that was right. Or even intelligent. They would have to change or they would fall as surely as this house. They should have started changing before this place was built. They should have . . . She became aware that it was light she stared at and felt a surge of hope. By now she guessed there would be people around unless the whole house fell, but she couldn't hear any voices. She called for help, but no one answered.

Slowly the morning light grew bright enough for her to see the place where she'd been sick and to push plaster dust and rubble over the worst of it. Each movement she made caused things to fall and scare her. Her head hurt. She was cold, and all her bones ached. A chipped front tooth scratched against her tongue. The right sleeves of her robe and pajamas had been ripped half off, and there was a deep ragged scratch on that arm, clotted and dirty.

Then from far away she heard a clanking, scraping noise and guessed it was a tractor of some sort, pushing through the ruin. At first she was excited, then it occurred to her that the tractor might crush her, or cause the rubble to shift and do so. She tried to shout, and the effort sent her into a choking spasm. When she could breathe again, she forced herself to calm down and see if she could save herself.

She appeared to be in a wedge-shaped space less than a foot

and a half high at the widest point. One wall of the wedge was the broken back of a massive credenza. The ceiling appeared to be part of a bedroom wall. Thin shafts of pale light poked through here and there, and what looked like mist in that light was dust.

Just ahead of her, where the bricks were, she could see an opening on the right. Without stopping to think about what might be on the other side, she shrugged off the ragged robe— it was sloppy and might catch on something. She ripped off the pajama sleeve, tied it on as a dust mask, then pushed her way forward. The wall above her creaked and snapped when she wormed between it and the brick pile. She stopped and then moved forward again; if she was going to die, she would die trying. There was gray light ahead when her hips stuck, and she had to back out and carefully move bricks and try again.

The gray light came from a hole where the surface she was crawling on had broken off and dropped. A few feet below was a jumble of smashed stucco and twisted reinforcing bars. And more light. Pushing forward, she tumbled shoulder first onto the pile, breaking the fall with her hands as best she could. Chunks dislodged by her weight broke loose and rolled. She held her breath, afraid she could slide, too.

She was near the top of a pile of rubble. Part of a roof bending over the pile capped and shaded this place like a dormer. Directly below was sunlight. She scooted down a few feet. Beyond stood the rest of the house, still intact. Only one wing had collapsed; the corridors leading into the wing gaped open like balconies without rails.

After looking for the best route, Merry climbed down the pile, stepping gingerly in bare feet, grabbing handholds where she could, skirting broken furniture, bathroom basins, tattered carpets limp as rags. She detoured around things that seemed too shaky and eventually reached the safety of the lawn and the luxury of grass beneath her feet. Even there she had to watch her step; the grass was littered with shards, and her left foot was quite painful.

Someone shouted over the noise of the tractor. She paid no attention. From her viewing point at ground level the tractor was hidden behind a mountain of rubble. What she saw now were the pine trees. Halfway down the grove were a fountain and pool. More than anything else right now she wanted water.

The water in the fountain basin was filmed with dust. Dirt had created a foam ring that shivered and danced in the splashing. She ignored that and drank from her hands, dismissing the dirt on them as well. Dirt was one of those things you worried about when everything else was all right. The water was cold and tasted of leaves.

"Meredith? Meredith? Where did you go?"

He was close by the time she heard him over the splash of the fountain. "Here!" she tried to say, but coughed instead. The cough served as a guide.

Afterward, when she remembered the expression on her grandfather's face, she realized that she'd never seen him really happy before. He came running down the slope, dodging trees, grinning like a boy, to swoop her up and hug her, saying, "You're alive! You're alive!" It was a good memory, the kind that gives one strength.

As he wrapped his jacket around her, her legs turned into noodles. She was staring down at their wobble when he picked her up bodily and started off toward the house. She was going to protest but lacked the energy. Other people came then; she was aware of them and of being put onto a stretcher and the stretcher being carried. She heard them asking how she was and her grandfather's answers, but suddenly a child's voice cut through the sunlight and concerned murmurs.

"Is that Merry? Is she dead?"

"Sami!"

H. M. Hoover

"Merry! Are you hurt bad?" Sami was beside the stretcher, walking backward part of the time to keep the sun out of her eyes.

"I don't think so—how did you get out?"

"I think I was thrown out. All of a sudden there wasn't any wall, and I was in some bushes, and I ran—I wanted to get help. Nobody knew we were in there. You saved me when nobody else could or would. And I wanted to help him, too—his song was so lonely. Like me . . . like he'd never get home again . . ."

"You heard him singing? That's why you ran off?" Merry asked.

"I *had* to—I know I promised, but I *had* to—I don't know why." Sami frowned as her mind danced to another thought. "But he was so scary when I found him—not like his song at all!"

"He doesn't matter now," the doctor said, and Merry saw a glance pass between her and the general, and the doctor nodded. "They just found the body."

After a bath and extensive first aid Merry slept the day away, as did her small houseguest. Sami went on sleeping while Merry and the general met for a late dinner and then went to the library to talk.

"Do you still believe Mikel came from Terra II?" she asked.

"I do. My staff does not. But then their education is lacking where history is concerned. It will take some time to convince them that we should even try to contact The Shepherd Moon. I wonder, is it worth the bother? The moons are moving farther away each minute—becoming more remote."

"Yes." She spoke without hesitation, and he smiled at her youthful surety.

"Then we'll do it." He thought a moment and sighed. "We might get to see inside that moon, after all . . . or I might

146

be gently eased from power as a crackpot."

"Or you might save a lot of lives."

"And if I fail to convince the Federation of the possible danger, you will be left with the burden of having to live down or overcome my ruined reputation." He smiled wryly. "Of course, you'll be able to live it down in very comfortable circumstances." He poured himself a drink, then settled back in his chair. "I know we discussed coming back here together in the spring, but I thought you might like to consider living with me on a more or less permanent basis." He was being deliberately casual. "After all, we seem to get along . . . and your parents travel quite a bit. We'll have to ask them, but do you think—"

"I'd like that!" Merry interrupted. "There's nothing I'd like better! I won't be a bother, and I won't talk when you don't want me to, and—" She was beginning to blither, thinking of how to please, not wanting to disappoint or bore him as she did her parents. And if they lived together, maybe she could make him understand and help, maybe they could change things.

"Then it's settled." He nodded to himself. "Yes, I think that would be best." He stood up and stretched as if tired from the long day.

On her way to bed she looked in on Sami and found the little girl awake. There was a plate with cake crumbs and an empty milk glass on a silver tray on the bedstand.

"I was waiting for you," Sami said. "I wanted to ask you—are we going home tomorrow?"

"Yes. After lunch, I think."

"What happens to me then?"

"Nothing . . ." The question startled Merry. It hadn't occurred to her that Sami might expect or worry about punishment, for that was what her tone and words implied. "You'll go back to school—but this time you have to study—"

"How do you know I didn't?"

"Because you're too smart," Merry said quickly, not wanting to say the general had access to all records.

"School's boring. If I fail again, do I get conscripted again?"

"No. But you shouldn't fail. If you do, I'll be disappointed."

"Will you know?"

"Yes." Merry looked her straight in the eye.

"Oh. Then I'll pass. I'll even pass Intermediate and try to go on to the university. I won't disappoint you. That's a promise. Merry?"

"Yes?"

"Will we ever see each other again? After tomorrow, I mean?"

The easy answer would have been "Yes, sure," and Merry nearly said it, but there was nothing sure about it, and honesty won out. "Probably not. Not for a long time. At least until we're both old enough not to have to take orders from other people. What do you think?"

"Probably not," Sami reluctantly agreed, and sighed as she thought of something. "To be honest, you wouldn't fit into my neighborhood—especially if they knew your grandfather was an officer. They hate officers . . . and so do I, mostly. And if they thought I had friends like you . . . You know how people are," she added apologetically.

Merry nodded but wasn't sure she did know.

"But no matter what," Sami went on, "I won't ever forget you—or this place, or anything."

"No," Merry promised, "I won't forget you either

With Merry gone, the general sat alone, staring into the fire. Almost abstractedly he reached into a pocket and pulled out jade beads strung on a fine gold chain. As he did so, a few grains of sand rumbled from the drill holes and spilled onto his trouser leg. He brushed the cloth and sat back, fingering the beads. They were the color of spring willows. Williams, coming in to clear away the glasses, saw him hastily pocket something and noted that there were tears running down his face. Each man ignored the other's presence.

ABOUT THE AUTHOR

H. M. Hoover is one of America's leading writers of science fiction for young people. She is the author of *The Delikon, The Rains of Eridan, The Lost Star, Return to Earth, This Time of Darkness,* and *The Bell Tree,* all published by Viking. Her book *Another Heaven, Another Earth* is an ALA Best Book.

Ms. Hoover lives near Washington, D.C., where she pursues her interests in natural history, archaeology, and history, as well as writing.